REYNARD THE FOX

ALSO BY JAMES SIMPSON

Under the Hammer:
Iconoclasm in the Anglo-American Tradition

Burning to Read:
English Fundamentalism and Its Reformation Opponents

Reform and Cultural Revolution
(volume 2 in *The Oxford English Literary History*)

REYNARD THE FOX

A NEW TRANSLATION

James Simpson

Illustrations by Edith E. Newman

LIVERIGHT PUBLISHING CORPORATION
A DIVISION OF W. W. NORTON & COMPANY
NEW YORK LONDON

Printed in the United States of America
First Edition

Manufacturing by Courier Westford
Book design by JAM Design
Production manager: Anna Oler

ISBN 978-0-87140-736-8

Liveright Publishing Corporation
500 Fifth Avenue, New York, N. Y. 10110
www.wwnorton.com

W. W. Norton & Company Ltd.
Castle House, 75/76 Wells Street, London W1T 3QT

1 2 3 4 5 6 7 8 9 0

I dedicate this translation to a great lover of animal stories, Jill Mann

Contents

✦

PART I

PART II

PART III

✦

PART IV

PART V

PART VI

PART VII

PART VIII

THE TRANSLATOR TAKES LEAVE OF HIS BOOK

Foreword

BY STEPHEN GREENBLATT

I would like to pretend to more learning than I possess by claiming that I had long known and admired William Caxton's 1481 translation from the Dutch of *Reynard the Fox*. But, though it goes against the spirit of the work's eponymous hero who lies gleefully about everything, I have to confess that I only just now encountered it for the first time. How happy I am that I have made its acquaintance, and still more that I have done so in James Simpson's wonderfully lively modernization! For though I would no doubt feel highly virtuous to have slogged my way through Caxton's quaint spelling and syntax, the truth is that this virtue is not altogether compatible with pleasure, and pleasure—sly, wicked, quick-witted, cynical pleasure—is the overarching theme of this remarkable work.

To be sure, the work is clearly a satire, one that exposes the greed, corruption, and lying that poison institutions and social relations, above all at court. It would appear then at least implicitly to take the side of virtue—scrupulous honesty, straightforwardness, hard work, and even-handed justice—against those like Reynard who make their way in the world by cunning and deceit. Yet like trickster tales in many languages and cultures, this one contrives to make the reader celebrate what he or she should rightly, that is, on strictly moral grounds, condemn. It does so in part by depicting the figures of authority—the Lion King and his counselors—as hopelessly flawed. They are not only dim-witted but also greedy, coarse, and self-interested, so that they can be all-too-easily manipulated. In part too this tale implies that Reynard's motives—to stuff his belly and to take care of his family at the expense of everyone else—are shared by all creatures. And in part it takes delight in sheer cleverness. Reynard the Fox is the animal fable's version of Homer's Odysseus, the man of many wiles. He possesses, far more than anyone else in his world, what the Greeks called *metis,* a blend of resourcefulness, expertise, and cunning that enables him to survive against all odds. And we applaud him for it.

The version of this figure with whom I grew up was Br'er Rabbit, in the stories that Joel Chandler Harris adapted from the African-American oral tradition. But that trickster rabbit seems benign and innocent compared to Reynard the Fox. For what strikes me most about the medieval tale is not the rich vein of laughter that James Simpson rightly celebrates but its unremitting cruelty. The hero is not only an inveterate liar but also a sadist, a rapist, and a murderer. Apart from his immediate family, anyone who comes too near him is grievously injured—scalded, bitten, scratched, mutilated, and (if tasty) eaten. It helps, of course, that this is an animal fable, so what might otherwise seem like pages taken from *King Lear* or *Othello* come across as episodes from a "Road Runner" cartoon or an episode of *The Itchy & Scratchy Show.* Still more, the literary artistry of *Reynard the Fox*—its pace, its deft twists of plot, its zany characters, and its savage humor—persuades us that to survive in this world it is more important to pretend to be good than actually to be good. To this extent at least, Reynard is the secret twin of his great contemporary Niccolò Machiavelli.

Introduction

iccolò Machiavelli's scandalous book *The Prince* was written in 1513 and published in 1532. Machiavelli wrote the book as counsel to princes and kings, but what continues to shock readers, even now, is the candor with which Machiavelli breaks from the long tradition of advice books to rulers. For many centuries prior to Machiavelli, classical and medieval philosophers had, that is, advised rulers to be virtuous. Machiavelli, by contrast, argues that virtue is insufficient. The fundamental need of the ruler is to preserve power, and the preservation of power demands more than virtue. In fact it also demands force and trickery.

Machiavelli's book continues to shock us even today. *The Prince*'s scandalous claim—that trickery was what was needed in politics—was, however, already at least three hundred years old by the time Machiavelli wrote in early sixteenth-century Florence. A set of literary narratives about the fox Reynard had been runaway best sellers since the late twelfth century. These racy animal stories celebrate survival through trickery. However, whereas Machiavelli had counseled kings to survive their enemies and subjects, *Reynard* is rather about how clever subjects can survive enemies and kings.

Machiavelli is explicitly conscious of animal literature and its value for teaching rulers. Thus Chapter 18 of *The Prince* begins by repeating the old advice that kings need to keep promises without trickery. That old advice, however, is contradicted by experience, since, as Machiavelli says, we need only look around us to see how successful rulers use trickery: they are "skillful in cunningly confusing men." So there are two ways for a ruler to act: either by observing laws (like men) or by using force (like animals). The problem is that observance of laws is "often ineffective," so the ruler must behave like the animals, and use force. That is a simple account of animal behavior, and Machiavelli knows it, for he immediately goes on to give a more subtle account of how different animals act to survive. The ruler should "act like a beast," to be sure, but "he should imitate the fox and the lion, for the lion is liable to be trapped, whereas the fox cannot ward off wolves."[1]

Machiavelli knows perfectly well, then, that if some animals rely on brute strength, others operate through trickery. In exactly the same way, the animal stories that flourished for the three centuries before Machiavelli, throughout Europe, represent different animals as either brutal or foxy, using either force or fraud. Brutal animals certainly populate the Reynard stories (for example, the wolf), but no reader admires or enjoys them. Readers do, however, enjoy observing Reynard at work, and that's because Reynard, as survivor-hero of these stories, never uses force, but only trickery. Brains—and very inventive brains at that—trump brawn every time. Reynard stories refuse, what's more, to keep the realm of human law separate from the realm of animal force, since all the Reynard narratives start from the court of the lion. Reynard is at his most brilliant in court, acting as a mercurial self-defense lawyer. He manipulates narrative in court to save himself and defeat his enemies, as he is "skillful in cunningly confusing" other animals. He wins not because he's virtuous (which he most certainly isn't), but rather because he's inventively clever. His outrageous tactics underline the point that humans are fooling themselves if they think the law is wholly *different* from the animal kingdom. On the contrary, the law is where the clever (human) animal can succeed best.

These astonishing, scandalous, deeply enjoyable fox stories had been available from the late twelfth century. When printing began in Europe in the mid–fifteenth century, enterprising publishers, in all the major European languages, certainly understood the attraction of the Reynard story: the list of Reynard publications in these languages, across that vast chronology from the beginning of printing to the twentieth century, is huge and of extraordinarily high quality. The Dutch verse text that lies, at a couple of removes, behind the translation presented here is, for example, "generally acknowledged to be one of the masterpieces—if not *the* masterpiece—of medieval Dutch literature."[2]

When I read *Reynard the Fox* for the first time in the early 1980s, I instantly knew that *Reynard* could be enjoyed by everyone over a certain age: the literary pleasures of this work are instantly accessible to all lovers of great narrative, of whatever age above, say, twelve. We are all political animals who need to survive, whatever we do. And all of us like laughing. And all of us are fascinated by animals, not least because we are ourselves animals who need to pretend otherwise.

And yet, and yet: the Reynard material presented here is not well known in English literature, not even among specialists.

The obvious explanation for this remarkable gap is that there is no readily available modern English text of Caxton's *Reynard the Fox.* No readily accessible English translation of the narrative presented here has, indeed, been available for almost a century.[3]

To appreciate the strikingly unsentimental candor and comedy of the Reynard stories, we need to step back from them a little to set them in the context of medieval animal stories. Medieval literature abounds in stories about animals, of which there are two main, easily distinguished varieties: animal fables and beast epic.[4] Animal fables claim Aesop as their source. They are small narratives in which animals act and speak, with even smaller morals tacked on at the end of the little stories. They involve many animals (such as mice, lambs, cocks, foxes, birds, wolves, lions, and frogs). Such stories were used to teach schoolboys both Latin and some commonsense morality into the bargain (like don't overeat; don't overreach; save up for the hard times; justice can be rough and ready, so keep clear of the predators).

Beast epic, by contrast, is a group of interconnected narratives, set in the court of the lion; its single hero is Reynard the Fox. Beast epic presents narratives of dark but vital humor that repeat the same narrative with many variations: its rhetorically brilliant fox Reynard outwits all comers by manipulating their bottomless greed. No matter how tight the corner into which Reynard has been backed, we know he'll escape. He'll escape through brilliant narrative control and intimate, intuitive knowledge of his enemies' weaknesses. He exposes the arrogance of the greedy, but even more damagingly the hypocrisy of the "civilized" order.

The Aesopic collections are much older than the Reynardian

stories. The Latin collection of Phaedrus (first century AD), a translation of a Greek "Aesop," represents the chief source of later fable collections. Phaedrus was paraphrased in a collection known as "Romulus" (ca. 350–500?), which was versified in the twelfth century. This collection is behind many of the vernacular Aesops of the later Middle Ages, including the *Aesop* (1484) printed by William Caxton, just three years after the publication of Caxton's *Reynard*, the text translated here.[5]

The Reynardian stories derive ultimately from Aesop: one of its central stories, the tale of the sick lion, in which the fox tricks the wolf, appears in Aesop. The continuous narrative characteristic of the Reynard material begins, however, with *The Escape of the Captive* (or *Ecbasis Captivi*, mid–eleventh century) and is greatly developed in the *Ysengrimus* (1148–49), an important source for the earliest branches of the French *Roman de Renart*.[6] The so-called "branches" of the *Roman de Renart* are short narrative sequences in French, composed probably between the 1170s and the middle of the thirteenth century.[7] These stories ultimately inspired many more adaptions in other Western European languages for the next 250 years and beyond, including Chaucer's brilliant *Nun's Priest's Tale* (1390s), sections of the equally brilliant *Moral Fables* (ca. 1475) of the Scots poet Robert Henryson, and the Flemish version from which Caxton translated his English text.[8]

In sum, at least two great traditions of animal stories are very widely attested in Europe from at least the eleventh century. Long before the invention of printing, there was an avid audience for stories about animals. Neither of these traditions told readers anything much they didn't already know about the nonhuman animal kingdom.[9] Their interest is definitely not that of natural history. Both traditions, however, teach us a great deal about human relations, by looking at the human kingdom from the angle of animals. Animals are like and unlike humans in myriad ways. In stories like these we cannot help thinking about ourselves as we contemplate the animal world.

What the Reynard stories teach us is not flattering, even if it's often funny and always revealing. Animal stories generally tend to work in two basic ways: they suggest either that animals are like humans, or that humans are like animals. When the animals are like humans, the stories are often cute, like Beatrix Potter's *The Tale of Peter Rabbit* (1901), in which we can instantly recognize the touching behavior of small children in the innocent adventures of Peter. If, by contrast, the suggestion is that humans are like animals, then the stories offer dark accounts of how humans are savage, like Book 4 of Swift's *Gulliver's Travels* (1726), where the humans are so savage as to suffer badly in comparison with more civilized animals. George Orwell's *Animal Farm* (1945) falls somewhere in the middle of these two extremes, since we feel sympathy for the humanlike suffering of some animals, and antipathy toward the heartless, unkind viciousness of others. Stories where the animals are like humans are generally for children, whereas stories where the humans are like animals are written for adults.

In that vast spectrum of animal stories, from the sweetly cute to the darkly satiric, *Reynard the Fox* definitely falls toward the darker end, for adults. But *Reynard* is unusual, insofar as it is not viciously satiric or shockingly savage, like Book 4 of *Gulliver's Travels.* We do not come away from *Reynard* like Gulliver coming away from his travels, filled with horror at human society. On the contrary, we come away laughing. William Caxton, the author of the text translated here, presented his *Reynard* as moral material for merchants and nobles to train their children ethically. In fact *Reynard* does nothing of the sort; but it does teach readers how to survive, or at least how not to fall victim, in the dog-eat-dog world of political, legal, and mercantile competition. We simultaneously learn about the world and how to survive in it. *Reynard* is most definitely not, therefore, for the very young, but young adult readers will enjoy and learn a lot.

The essential, and the rather mysterious, thing is that some of these stories make us laugh. It's mysterious because Reynard is a selfish, pitiless confidence trickster. Readers will decide for themselves if and how these stories are funny, but a translator needs to make some attempt to unlock the mystery of this scandalous, apparently amoral comedy.

No one likes or admires a confidence trickster. But what if the trickster is astonishingly clever as he tricks his victims? He knows, for example, exactly what will flatter or allure his victims at any given moment. Well, we might say, we can stand back and admire (if that's the right word) the cunning, even if we continue to feel pity for the victims.

But in addition to the trickster's skill, we might note that the trickster's victims are greedy. Through their greed, these victims also become stupid, incapable of seeing the trap that stares them in the face. Once we recognize the victim's greed and resultant stupidity, the potential for enjoying the trickster at work improves, since we feel no pity for most of the victims. If we did feel pity for a story's victims, we would see the fox as a wolflike predator, stalking and consuming the innocent. Such a narrative would be primarily a story of society's victims. We'd grieve as we read. But if we don't feel pity, and if the victims are indeed brutal, greedy, and stupid, then our reading will take a different turn: we might, that is, see amusing comeuppance for the obtuse and greedy. The effect of the story is transformed, as it becomes a story of society's brilliant outsider and victor. It's no longer the story of the wolflike predator (and there is one of these in *Reynard*, called Isengrim the Wolf) so much as the story of foxy genius exploiting the deserving dumb. We might start laughing as we read.

Before we can really appreciate our trickster's genius, however, we need also to see that the victims are often also *themselves* predators. They are, in fact, no less predatory than the obvious predator, even if they are infinitely less clever, and even if they hypocritically dress their predations up as law, learning, and religion. Their predations are often, in fact, plain brutal. The victims are greedy, obtuse, hypocritical, and often cruel. So the predator fox becomes a hero, or antihero of sorts, since he's wonderfully clever, makes no claim to moral superiority, and for the most part cheats only stupid, greedy, predatory, and often brutal hypocrites. Not only that, but he cheats them repeatedly, since their readiness to fall victim to greed is infinite. The Reynard-centered, beast-epic stories prompt us, that is, to scrutinize the solidity of the "civilized" order. For once that order has been created by animals, we cannot help but see through its pretensions, since most animals, and certainly the big ones who make the rules (like us, for example), are often predators and carnivores.

As soon as printing was invented in the mid–fifteenth century, publishers saw potential sales in the Reynard stories. In England, for example, William Caxton, England's first printer, translated, printed, and marketed wickedly funny *Reynard the Fox.*

Caxton was near the front of the information technology revolution of the fifteenth century. He did not invent anything, but he did capitalize on the invention of printing to translate, make, and sell books in an entirely new format, at a lower price, for much larger numbers of readers in Britain.

Caxton was born between 1415 and 1424, probably in Kent. He had been apprenticed to a London mercer (a trader in fine textiles) in 1438, but by the latter half of the 1440s had moved across the channel to the heart of the cloth trade, in Bruges, the still beautiful city in modern-day Belgium, then part of the Duchy of Flanders. Bruges was simultaneously a political center for the Dukes of Burgundy, and a center of trade. It had a very large population and a kind of stock exchange—when the Parisian merchant in Chaucer's *The Shipman's Tale* (1390s) needs to trade on the money market, he goes to Bruges. Caxton flourished there: between 1462 and 1470 he served as the governor of the English Nation (that is, the leader of the organization representing English commercial and political interests).

In Bruges, Caxton was at the heart of an international trading center, which brought him into contact with flows of information, technical advancements, and luxury goods (such as spices, armor, silks, exotic fruits, and luxury manuscript books) from all over Europe and the wider Mediterranean. It also brought him into contact with the new technology of printing.

At the same time that Caxton was on the lookout for business in Bruges, Johannes Gutenberg published his first book with movable type, the Gutenberg Bible, in about 1455, in Mainz, central western Germany. (It had been independently invented in China and Korea from the eleventh century CE.) Until Gutenberg's mid–fifteenth-century invention, each book in Europe had to be composed, and then copied, laboriously and expensively, by hand in manuscripts (*manu-script*, or "hand-written").

In the decades of the 1460s and '70s, Gutenberg's invention spread quickly through Western and Central Europe,[10] and one can see why: suddenly the extraordinarily expensive business of reproducing books, in very small numbers, for elite audiences had become relatively cheap; and printers could produce many more books than was imaginable in a manuscript culture. Thanks to this totally transformative technology, a new culture of literacy was about to take off in Europe. Every area of social life, be it commerce, religion, law, politics, education, medicine, or literature, for example, would soon be utterly transformed by the introduction of printing. The cultural transformation was easily as profound as the one we are currently experiencing in the digital age.

Setting up a printing press was, however, extremely expensive. It required bold entrepreneurial spirits, such as William Caxton. As we have seen, Caxton was perfectly placed geographically to introduce a wholly new technology into England. From Bruges he went two hundred or so miles east to Cologne in 1471, where he not only learned to set up type but also bought the equipment he needed to establish a press in Bruges, before moving soon to England, where he published books from 1476.[11]

Caxton was also perfectly placed socially to judge the books that would sell well. The books he chose to print were not exactly new, and appealed to upper-class taste. Caxton's literary choices for his radically new technology derived initially, that is, from the trade network that had produced luxury manuscript books. These books included texts drawn from classical antiquity designed for aristocratic readers and buyers. Thus Caxton's first printed book (and the first book printed in English) was, for example, a history of the Trojan War by a French author Raoul Lefèvre, which Caxton himself had translated. Caxton produced his translation

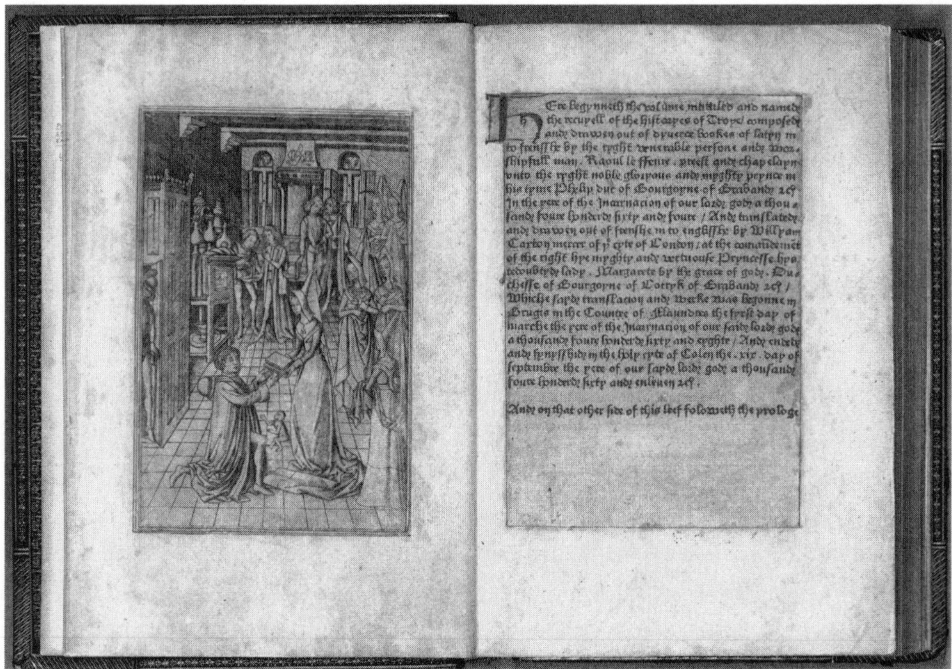

Here begynneth the volume intituled and named the recuyell of the historyes of Troye/ composed and drawen out of dyuerce bookes of latyn in to frensshe by the ryght venerable persone and worshipfull man. Raoul le ffeure. preest and chapelayn vnto the ryght noble gloryous and myghty prynce in his tyme Phelip duc of Bourgoyne of Braband &c In the yere of the Incarnacion of our lord god a thousand foure honderd sixty and foure / And translated and drawen out of frenshe in to englisshe by Willyam Caxton mercer of yͤ cyte of London / at the comaundemēt of the right hye myghty and vertuouse Pryncesse hys redoubtyd lady. Margarete by the grace of god. Duchesse of Bourgoyne of Lotryk of Braband &c / Whiche sayd translacion and werke was begonne in Brugis in the Countre of Flaundres the fyrst day of marche the yere of the Incarnacion of our said lord god a thousand foure honderd sixty and eyghte / And ended and fynysshid in the holy cyte of Colen the .xix. day of septembre the yere of our sayd lord god a thousand foure honderd sixty and enleuen &c.

And on that other syde of this leef foloweth the prologe

FIGURE 1: Raoul Lefèvre, *The recuyell of the historyes of Troye*, translated by William Caxton (Bruges, 1473), f. A1v, A2. HUNTINGTON LIBRARY, SAN MARINO, CALIFORNIA

in consultation with Margaret of Burgundy (1446–1503), sister of Edward IV of England and third wife of Charles the Bold, Duke of Burgundy. The frontispiece shows Caxton presenting his very new technological product in a very old and traditional posture: an author on his knees presents his book to an aristocratic patron.[12] One might also observe that the technology of reproduction might be new, but the "interface" of the book is very traditional: the printer has gone out of his way to make the page look like that of a handwritten book (Figure 1).

By December 1476, Caxton had moved back to England,

where he set up his press. He did not choose to set up operations in England's business center, the city of London. Instead, he established himself as a printer a few miles to the west of London, in Westminster. That choice set him near the great monastic abbey, but, more to the commercial point, right beside the royal court and Parliament. In this violent and turbulent period of continuing civil war in England (the so-called Wars of the Roses [1455–1485]), Caxton positioned himself to inform, counsel, and entertain his professional urban and aristocratic readers, and to make money. He accordingly published ninety-seven books from that press, many of which are very substantial. He published books of religious piety, chivalry (including Sir Thomas Malory's *Le Morte d'Arthur* in 1485), political advice, statutes, history, and works of relatively recent English literature, such as Chaucer's late fourteenth-century *Canterbury Tales* (two editions, published 1478 and 1484), and *Troilus and Criseyde* (published 1484). In both Bruges and Westminster, Caxton issued a total of 103 publications. Of these he translated at least 22 works, plus 4 other translations published by others, from French, Latin, and Dutch.[13]

Many of the books Caxton published are in the two largest and best-known traditions of medieval literature—chivalric literature and religious instruction. These promote, respectively, chivalric idealism and piety. The chilvalric idealism is not necessarily irrelevant to Caxton's own modernity: even if the narrative of Thomas Malory's *Le Morte d'Arthur* was, for example, set in the sixth-century Britain of King Arthur, it was about civil war, and was therefore directly relevant to England's own mid–fifteenth-century civil war. That said, Malory's book is nostalgic and tragic, looking back to another time in the distant past of great yet failed idealism.

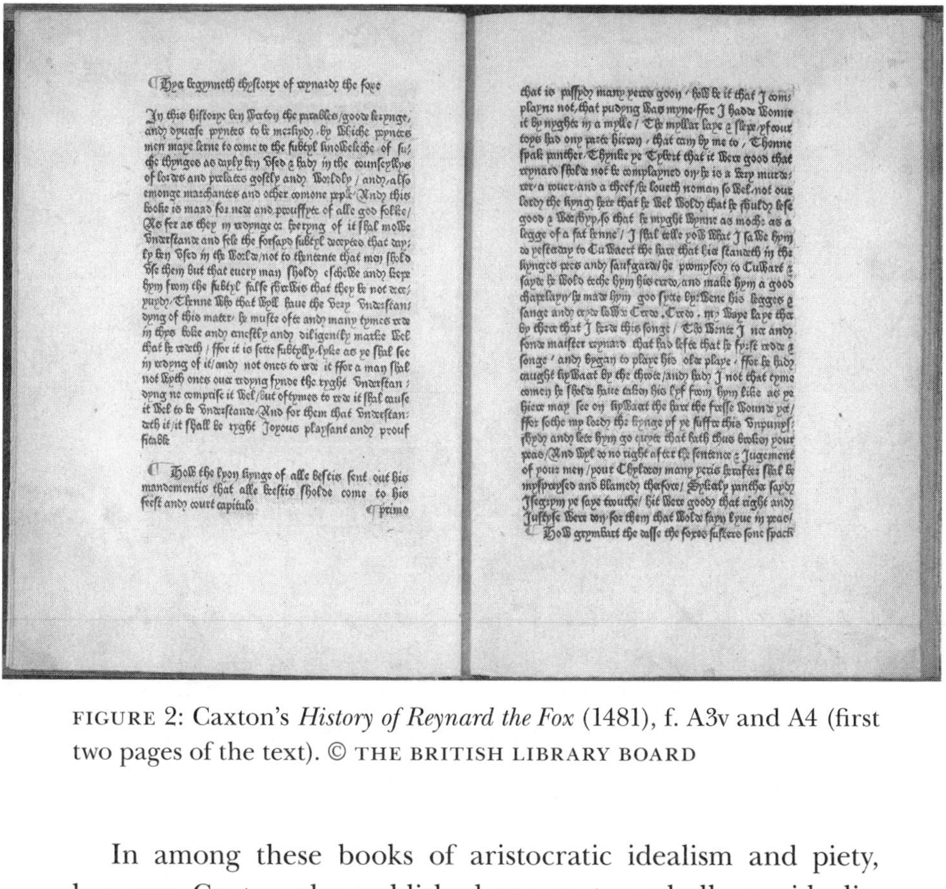

FIGURE 2: Caxton's *History of Reynard the Fox* (1481), f. A3v and A4 (first two pages of the text). © THE BRITISH LIBRARY BOARD

In among these books of aristocratic idealism and piety, however, Caxton also published one or two wholly nonidealistic, trenchantly unmoralistic works that present the world of the court in wholly unflattering and satirical ways. The greatest of these works is his *History of Reynard the Fox*, published first in 1481 (Figure 2), the book translated here as *Reynard the Fox.*

Caxton, whose publishing choices were for the most part cautious, chose to publish this astonishing, outrageous, mordant book because it was, in the first instance, clearly a reliable seller.

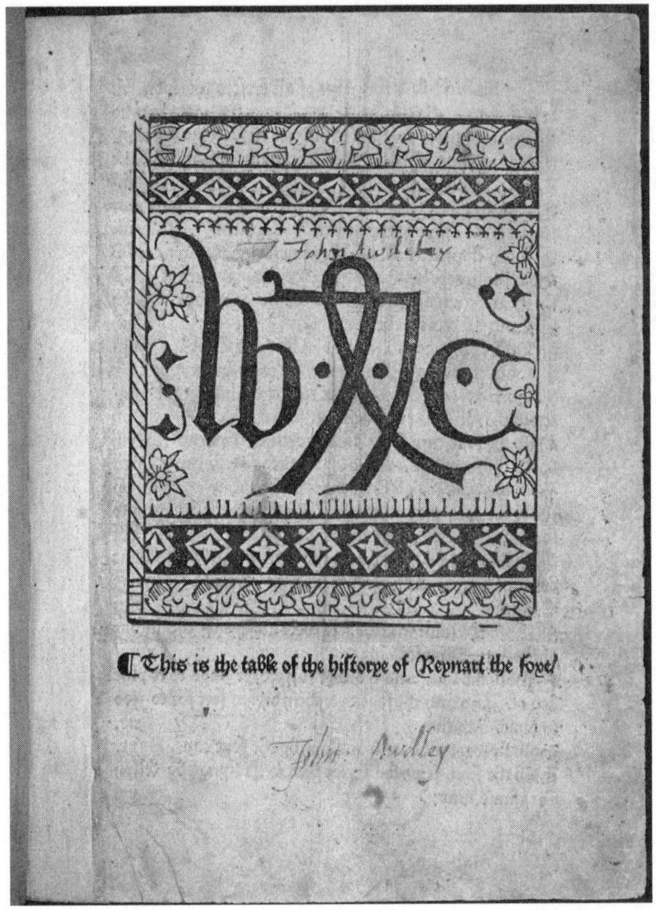

FIGURE 3: Frontispiece to Caxton's *History of Reynard the Fox* (London, 1489). PEPYS LIBRARY, MAGDALENE COLLEGE, CAMBRIDGE

It already had a long history of commercial success behind it in the Low Countries. Caxton translated his *History of Reynard the Fox* (1481) from Gerard Leeu's Flemish prose version *Reinaerts historie.* The Flemish version appeared in 1479, Caxton's

English version two years later. Leeu's text was itself an adaptation of an earlier Flemish version of the Reynard stories, *Reinaerts historie* (ca. 1375). This, in turn, had been translated from a mid–thirteenth-century Middle Dutch verse text, *Van den vos Reynaerde.*[14] And Caxton's English text was clearly a commercial success, since it was reprinted by Caxton himself in 1489 (with Caxton's magnificent business logo [Figure 3], and by one of Caxton's successor printers in London, Richard Pynson, in 1494, 1500–06, and 1525. The fact that there were a total of twenty-three Reynard editions published in England between 1481 and 1700 demonstrates that it was a runaway best seller.

But *Reynard the Fox* was also a seller because it answered to the intensely competitive, materialist conditions in which Caxton himself prospered, no less than it answers to our own times.

NOTES

1 Machiavelli, *The Prince,* edited by Quentin Skinner and Russell Price (Cambridge: Cambridge University Press, 1988), p. 61. I am grateful to Laura Wang for pointing me to Machiavelli's reference to the fox.

2 Jill Mann, review of *Of Reynaert the Fox: Text and Facing Translation of the Middle Dutch Beast Epic* Van den Vos Reynaerde, edited by André Bouwman and Bart Besamusca, in *Reynardus: Yearbook of the International Reynard Society* 22 (2010): 198–203 (at p. 198).

3 See *The Most Delectable History of Reynard the Fox,* edited by Joseph Jacobs (London and New York: Macmillan, 1895). For a Middle English version, see William Caxton, *The History of Reynard the Fox,* ed. N. F. Blake, EETS, 263 (London: Oxford University Press, 1970).

4 For a survey of medieval beast literature, with bibliographical guide, see Jill Mann, "Beast Epic and Fable," in *Medieval Latin: An Introduction and Bibliographical Guide,* ed. F. A. C. Mantello and A. G. Rigg (Washington, 1996), pp. 556–61. For a complete list of the branches of the *Roman de Renart,* see J. R. Simpson, *Animal Body, Literary Corpus: The Old French "Roman de Renart"* (Amsterdam: Rodopi, 1996), Appendix One. For a brief survey of the British animal material prior to Caxton's *Reynard,*

see N. F. Blake, "Reynard the Fox in England," in *Aspects of the Medieval Animal Epic: Proceedings of the International Conference, Louvain, May 15–17, 1972*, ed. E. Rombauts and A. Welkenhuysen (Louvain: Louvain University Press, 1975), pp. 53–65. The best critical book on medieval animal material is Jill Mann, *From Aesop to Reynard: Beast Literature in Medieval England* (Oxford: Oxford University Press, 2009).

5 William Caxton, *Caxton's Aesop*, ed. R. T. Lenaghan (Harvard: Harvard University Press, 1967).

6 This paragraph is drawn from James Simpson, "Beast Epic and Fable," in Paul E. Szarmach, M. Teresa Tavormina, and Joel T. Rosenthal, eds. *Medieval England: An Encyclopaedia* (New York, 1998), pp. 111–12. For the extraordinarily powerful and brilliant *Ysengrimus*, see *Ysengrimus*, ed. and trans. Jill Mann (Leiden: Brill, 1987).

7 For a survey of the entire medieval Reynard tradition, see John Flinn, *Le Roman de Reynart dans la littérature française et dans les littératures étrangères au moyen âge* (Toronto: University of Toronto Press, 1963), and Simpson, *Animal Body, Literary Corpus: The Old French "Roman de Renart,"* Appendix One.

8 For a brief summary and further references, see Mann, *From Aesop to Reynard: Beast Literature in Medieval England*, pp. 19–20.

9 For medieval texts that do respect the autonomy of animals, see Susan Crane, *Animal Encounters: Contacts and Concepts in Medieval Britain* (Philadelphia: University of Pennsylvania Press, 2013).

10 For which see the excellent table and map at http://en.wikipedia.org/wiki/Spread_of_the_printing_press, consulted 4 April 2014.

11 See N. F. Blake, *Caxton and His World* (London: Andre Deutsch, 1969), p. 56.

12 Raoul Lefèvre, *The recuyell of the historyes of Troye*, translated by William Caxton (Bruges, 1473).

13 For a complete bibliography of Caxton's output, see Blake, *Caxton and His World*, pp. 224–39.

14 *Van den Vos Reynaerde*, edited by André Bouwman and Bart Besamusca (Amsterdam: Amsterdam University Press, 2009). This text presents the Middle Dutch and English facing page translation.

A Note on the Translation

Translations classically address themselves primarily to one of two targets: either to the source text, where the aim is to reproduce that text as accurately as possible in the language of the translation; or to the audience, where the aim is to render the source text as delightfully and intelligibly as possible for the intended new audience. These aims are not, of course, wholly exclusive, but a translator must give priority to one or the other. I have a philological translation of Caxton's *Reynard* aimed at the source text in my files. The translation produced here is, however, of the second type. It's designed to reproduce the pleasure of the text for a new audience. Of course that second kind of translation will also stay as close to the original as the interests of the new audience will permit. This translation does not, in my view, betray the original at any point, even if I have attempted to render Caxton's prose in a more welcome idiom.

REYNARD
THE FOX

Animal Dramatis Personae

MAJOR PLAYERS

(in order of appearance)

Reynard the Fox

Isengrim the Wolf, *enemy to Reynard*

King Noble the Lion

SIGNIFICANT MINOR PLAYERS

(in order of appearance)

Courtoys the Dog: *a victim of Reynard's theft*

Tybert the Cat: *a victim of Reynard's cunning*

Cuwaert the Hare: *eaten by Reynard*

Grimbart the Badger: *Reynard's "nephew" and supporter*

Chaunticleer the Cock: *along with his family, a victim of Reynard*

Bruin the Bear: *despite his strength, an easy victim of Reynard*

Ermilyn: *wife of Reynard the Fox*

Bellin the Ram: *through stupidity a victim of Reynard*

The Lion Queen: *sympathetic to Reynard*

Arswind: *wife of Isengrim the Wolf, a victim of Reynard in various ways*

Fineskin the Leopard: *a supporter of Reynard in court*

Lapreel the Rabbit: *almost killed by Reynard*

Corbant the Crow: *his wife Sharpbeak is eaten by Reynard*

Mertin the Ape: *a friend of Reynard in the papal court*

Rukenawe the She-Ape: *a clever and powerful friend of Reynard in court*

Byteluys the Ape: *a supporter of Reynard*

PART I

Reynard the Fox is summoned to the court of the lion king, three times, to face charges. Two of the messengers learn the hard way not to mess with the fox

1

The lion, King of all beasts, commands all animals to come to his feast and his court

he woods were fresh, the trees adorned with blossoms, and the ground covered with herbs and sweet-smelling flowers. The birds sang harmoniously. It was the feast of Pentecost![1] The lion, noble King of all beasts, wished to hold open court over the days of the feast.

Summons to court was made throughout his realm, and every animal was commanded to appear. All beasts came, both great and small, except Reynard the Fox. Reynard knew that he was guilty on many counts involving other animals who would appear at court. So he didn't dare show up.

1 In Christianity, the religious feast of Pentecost commemorates the descent of the Holy Spirit to the Apostles and others fifty days after Easter (see Acts 2:1–31).

2

The first accusation against Reynard, made by Isengrim the Wolf

Isengrim the Wolf came with his family and supporters and stood in front of the King. "High and mighty prince, my lord King, I beg this of you: that by your great power, justice, and mercy, you'll pity me, given the seriousness of the crimes that Reynard the Fox has committed against me and my wife. He entered my house against my wife's will, and relieved himself on my children so as to blind them! He and I agreed on a day when Reynard should come to excuse himself for this crime and swear by the holy saints that he wasn't guilty of it. But when the book of the saints was brought out, Reynard had second thoughts: he returned to his hole, as if he didn't care a thing about the matter. Dear King, many of the animals here at your court know this to be true. And yet Reynard has wronged me in many other respects too: no man alive could tell you all that I now leave untold. But I swear to avenge the shame he's inflicted on my wife. For that he'll pay, and dearly!"

3

The accusation of Courtoys the Dog

fter this speech, a little dog named Courtoys stood up and complained to the King. In the cold winter, when the frost was hard and he'd been starved, he had nothing but a sausage left. Reynard stole it from him.

Then Tybert the Cat spoke up. He advanced angrily, springing among them. "My lord the King, I hear that Reynard is accused of serious crimes. No one present has more to do to clear his name. The matter Courtoys complains about happened many years ago, and even if I don't lay charges, that sausage was mine. I'd got it one night at a mill, when the miller was fast asleep. If Courtoys had any claim to it, it came through me."

Then the panther spoke. "Tybert, maybe we should accuse Reynard: he's a murderer, a scavenger, and a thief. He cares more about eating the leg of a fat hen than he does about the love of anyone here—even our lord the King—and he's prepared to lose his reputation and honor for it.

"I'll tell you what I saw him do only yesterday to Cuwaert the Hare, who stands here by the King's protection. Reynard promised Cuwaert that he'd teach him his Apostles' Creed and make him a virtuous chaplain.[2] Reynard required Cuwaert to sit between his legs and sing, crying out, '*Credo, Credo.*'[3]

"I happened to be passing by, and I heard the song. I came nearer and saw that Master Reynard couldn't care less about what he'd begun reading and singing. Instead, he began to play his old tricks, for he'd caught Cuwaert by the throat.

"If I hadn't been passing, he would've killed Cuwaert then and there: just look, you can see the wound still fresh on him. Truly, my lord King, you must on no account allow this crime to go unpunished and permit the criminal Reynard to go scot-free. If you don't exact justice according to the judgment of your own men, this is what'll happen: your children will be criticized and blamed on account of this for many years to come."

"Truly, panther," said Isengrim, "you're telling the truth: it's right that justice be done, for those who want only to live in peace."

2 The Apostles' Creed is one of the statements of belief for the early Christian Church.

3 "I believe, I believe." "Credo" is the first word of the Latin form of the Apostles' Creed.

4

Grimbart the Badger, the fox's nephew, speaks up for Reynard, in the presence of the King

Grimbart the Badger was Reynard's sister's son. He spoke angrily: "Sir Isengrim, you're malicious. It's a common proverb that an enemy's mouth seldom speaks well, and the charge you lay against my Uncle Reynard proves it. I wish you'd agree to this: that whoever of you two has sinned most against the other should hang by the neck like a thief on a tree. If Reynard were as tight with the King as you are with this court, he'd not consider it sufficient that you merely begged his forgiveness. You have bitten my uncle with your frightening teeth more times than I can tell.

"All the same, I'll go over some incidents that I know well. Don't you remember the fish Reynard threw down from the fisherman's basket, when you followed from afar? You ate the delicious fish alone, giving him no more than the skeleton and bones that you couldn't eat. You did the same thing with the fat slice of bacon that tasted so good. When my uncle inquired about his share, you answered him scornfully: 'Pretty young Reynard, I'll gladly give you your part,' but Uncle Reynard didn't get a scrap.

And he's the one who'd courageously won the bacon, since the man had thrown him in a sack, so that he barely escaped with his life.[4] Reynard has suffered many such episodes because of Isengrim.

"My lords! Does this strike you as right? Yet there's more! Isengrim also complains that my Uncle Reynard has wronged him by mistreating his wife. It's true that my uncle had some dalliance with her, but that was seven years ago, before Isengrim was married! And if Reynard treated her lovingly and courteously, what's the harm in that? She was soon over it. There should be no accusation whatsoever about this incident. Were Isengrim a wise man, he would've let it go. He gains no honor by slandering his wife in this way, and she herself makes no accusation.

"But now Cuwaert the Hare also makes an accusation, which seems to me ill-advised: if he failed to learn his lesson, shouldn't Reynard his master beat him? If scholars weren't beaten and told off for their laziness, they'd never learn!

"And then Courtoys the Dog complains—Courtoys, of all animals! He'd got hold of a sausage in winter, when such things are hard to come by. Courtoys would've been smarter to have kept quiet here, since he'd stolen the sausage in the first place: *male quaesisti, male perdidisti*![5] It's only right that what was ill-gained be ill-lost. Who'll blame Reynard, if he took stolen goods from a thief? Whoever understands the law and can tell right from wrong knows that Reynard was in the right. And whoever is as wellborn as Uncle Reynard knows how to handle stolen goods. No nobleman would think it remotely wrong or illegal if Rey-

4 These are both stories recounted in other branches of the Reynard material.

5 "You acquired it badly, you badly lost it."

nard had hanged Courtoys when he found him with the sausage. The only reason for not hanging him would be to avoid insult to the crown. So, not wanting to do justice without permission, and out of respect for the King, Reynard didn't hang Courtoys. And what's his reward for this? Not a thing! What wounds him most is that *he's* the one being accused.

"My Uncle Reynard is a noble and honest creature. He detests falsehood of any kind. He does nothing without the advice of his priest. I declare it openly that, since my lord the King proclaimed his peace, Reynard has never intended harm to a soul. He eats only once a day, and lives as a recluse. He punishes his body and wears a hair shirt. It's more than a year since he's eaten flesh. And as those said who came from him just now, he's abandoned and given up his castle Wickedhole. He's built a hermitage for himself, where he now lives. No more hunting, no more lust for flesh. Instead, he lives by charity and takes nothing but what men give him out of charity, doing continual penance for his sins. He's become pale and lean from praying and self-disciplining vigils. Peace with God is all he wants."

As Grimbart, Reynard's nephew, stood and delivered this speech, the court saw Chaunticleer the Cock coming down the hill. He carried a dead hen on a bier. Reynard had bitten its head off, and the evidence had to be shown to the King, so he'd know the truth.

The court saw Chaunticleer the Cock coming down the hill.
He carried a dead hen on a bier.

5

The cock accuses Reynard

Chaunticleer stepped up and piteously clapped his hands and feathers together. On each side of the coffin walked two sorrowful hens, Cantart and the good hen Crayant. They were the two prettiest hens between Holland and the Ardennes. Each bore a burning candle, which was long and straight. These hens were Coppen's sisters. They wept and wept: "We grieve for our dear sister Coppen!"

Two young hens bore the bier, and they cackled and wept so loudly because of the death of Coppen their mother that you could hear their wailing from miles away. They all came in front of the King.

Chaunticleer spoke for them: "Merciful lord, my lord the King, please hear our accusation. You'll be shocked by the frightful damage that Reynard has inflicted upon me and my children, who stand here before you!

"It was in the beginning of April, when the weather was beautiful. I was feeling courageous and proud, partly because I'm so nobly born, and partly because I had eight handsome sons and seven beautiful daughters hatched by my wife. All were strong and plump, and all protected by a well-walled yard. There were six huge guard dogs in a shed. They'd torn the skin from many animals, and so my own children were unafraid. Reynard the thief cast a greedy eye at my family, since they were so complacently certain that he couldn't touch them.

"How often has this fearsome thief crept carefully around our wall and lay in wait for us! How often have the dogs been set on him to chase him away! They once leapt on him by the riverbank, which cost him for his theft. I saw his skin smoking from the bite, but he escaped all the same. I hope God repays him someday.

"So we were free of Reynard for a long while, until finally he came dressed like a religious hermit. He brought me a letter to read, sealed by the King himself. This letter declared that the King had made peace throughout his realm, and that no beast or bird should harm or damage any other. What's more, Reynard said to me that he'd become a monastic recluse, and announced that he would undertake serious penance for his sins. He showed me his pilgrim's coat, with his fur and hair shirt beneath it.[6]

" 'Sir Chaunticleer,' he went on, 'you have no need to fear me anymore. Take no special notice of me, for I'll never eat flesh again. I've grown so old that I'd rather work on the fate of my soul. I'll now say goodbye, for I've yet to say my monastic prayers for midday, midafternoon, and evensong.'[7]

"So Reynard left, saying his creed. He then hid himself under a hedge. Relieved and delighted, I forgot my anxieties and went

6 Reynard hypocritically pretends to be a religious pilgrim, who undertakes an arduous pilgrimage as a form of punishment for sins committed, in the hope of pardon.

7 Reynard pretends to be performing the so-called canonical hours, prayers to be made in monastic communities at set times of the day and night.

to my children and clucked them all together, after which I foolishly took them for a stroll outside my wall. Bad things follow from such thoughtless behavior, for Reynard came creeping between us and the gate. He snatched one of my children and stuffed him in his pouch, which has caused us such terrible grief. For after he'd tasted just one chick, no hunter or dog could keep him from all of us. He's lain in wait night and day so cunningly that he's stolen many of my children. Of fifteen, I have only four left! The thief has killed them!

"And just yesterday the body of Coppen my daughter, who lies here upon this bier, was recovered by the dogs. I lay this charge in your presence, gracious King, that you might take pity on me for the unreasonable harm I've suffered through the loss of my children."

6

The King calls for counsel

he King spoke: "Sir badger, listen to this latest charge against your uncle the hermit: if I live a year he'll pay dearly, despite all his praying and fasting!

"Now listen to me, Sir Chaunticleer: Your accusation is sufficient. Your daughter we give over to death, since we can't bring her back to life. We entrust her to God, as we sing her vigil mass and bury her reverently. We'll then take counsel among these lords, deciding how we might best enforce justice for this terrible murder, and how we might bring this false thief to law."

Then they began the service for the dead (*Placebo domino*),[8] with the appropriate verses, which would take me too long to repeat now. When the requiem mass had ended, she was buried, with a marble gravestone polished as brightly as any mirror, in which an epitaph in large letters had been incised:

> **Coppen, Chaunticleer's daughter, whom Reynard the Fox bit, lies buried here. Lament her death, for she was shamefully murdered.**

8 "I will please the Lord." An abbreviated form of the Office of the Dead, drawn from a Psalm text (Vulgate 114:9).

The King then sent for his lords and the wisest of his council, to deliberate on Reynard the Fox's punishment for this dreadful murder. The beasts concluded that they should send for Reynard. There was no way he could evade a summons to appear in the King's court and hear judgment against him.

They also decided that Bruin the Bear should be the messenger.

All this seemed good and proper to the King, who addressed Bruin the Bear: "Sir Bruin, I want you to carry this message. But take good care of yourself, for Reynard is wicked and dangerous. He has lots of tricks up his sleeve, and he'll lie, flatter, and do nothing but ponder how he can deceive and mock you."

Bruin replied: "Good lord, it'd be a bit late in the day for the fox to deceive me! I've learned my law cases. I think he comes too late to make a fool of me."

Thus Bruin left merrily. We can all regret that he didn't return in quite so merry a mood.

7

How Bruin the Bear fares with Reynard the Fox

ow Bruin was on his way to the fox, fully convinced that the fox couldn't outwit him. He entered a dark forest, into which Reynard tended to take a side track when he was being hunted. Beside it were a high mountain and a clearing, which Bruin had to traverse on his way to Wickedhole. Reynard had many escape holes, but Wickedhole was the best and most secure. He hid there whenever he needed to, and whenever he was afraid.

Now, when Bruin arrived at Wickedhole, he found the gate securely shut. So he went and sat upon his tail in front of the gate.

"Reynard, are you at home? It's Bruin here! The King has sent me to you. You must come to court to plead your case. The King has sworn by God that if you don't come, or if I fail to bring you with me to receive sentence, you're a dead man. He'll either hang you or set you on the wheel. Reynard, do as I suggest: come to court!"

Reynard lay just within the gate enjoying the sun, as he often did, when he heard Bruin. He went directly into a hole. Wickedhole was full of holes—here one and there another, and over there yet another narrow, crooked, and long hole with many exits. Reynard opened and shut these according to need. Whenever he brought prey home, or whenever he knew that anyone was after him for his crimes, he ran into his secret chambers. There he hid from his enemies so that they couldn't find him. In this way he'd tricked many beasts that had tried to capture him. So Reynard reflected on how best to bamboozle the bear, and how to save trouble for himself.

He emerged from his hole: "Welcome, Uncle Bruin![9] I heard you before, but I was saying my prayers for evensong, and so tarried a little, dear uncle. Whoever sent you over this long hill did you no favors. I can't thank him, for I see that you're so exhausted that the sweat is running down your face. Your trip is completely unnecessary, since I was coming to court tomorrow. But I'm happy you've come all the same, because your wise counsel will help me in court. Couldn't the King find some less important messenger than you? That's amazing, because, apart from the King, you're the noblest and wealthiest figure in court.

"I wish we were already at court, but I'm afraid I won't be able to come just now, for I've eaten so much food that I fear my stomach will burst. The food was new to me, which made me eat more of it."

"Dear nephew, what food was it that's filled you up?"

"Dear uncle, how would it help you if I told you what I ate? I eat but simple food. A poor man is no lord—you can see that in

9 Reynard frequently calls other animals with no possible family relation to him "uncle" or "aunt." He does this to insinuate intimacy and trust. More often than not, the animals whom he addresses in this way will soon become his victims.

me. We poor folk must oftentimes eat what we'd prefer not to, if we had better food. They were great honeycombs that I was obliged to eat because of hunger. They've made my belly so great that I'm afraid I'll burst."

Bruin answered immediately: "Reynard, what on earth are you talking about? Do you think honey is so worthless? We ought to praise and love honey as the very best of foods! Dear Reynard, help me get a great swag of that honey. I'll be a true friend and stick with you if you help me to have just a part of it."

8

Bruin eats the honey

"Uncle Bruin, I think you're pulling my leg."

"So help me God, Reynard, no. I wouldn't joke around with you!"

So Reynard replied: "Is it true, then, that you love honey so much? I'll give you enough honey that ten bears wouldn't be able to eat it at one meal. But there's one condition: that I can secure your friendship."

"Don't say ten bears, nephew Reyner," said the bear; "that wouldn't work at all: if I had all the honey between here and Portugal, I'd gobble it up all alone."

"Okay, so here's the deal. There's a farmer called Lantfert who lives next door. He's got so much honey that you couldn't eat it in seven years. It's all yours, if you're prepared to be my friend and help me against my enemies at court."

Bruin the Bear promised him: if his belly was full, he'd be loyal to him above everyone else, for sure. Reynard the trickster laughed at this: "Okay, if you're after seven barrels of honey, they're yours. Leave it to me."

This pleased the bear so well and made him laugh so much that he could hardly stand. Reynard thought to himself all the while: *Things are going swimmingly; I'll lead him where he'll be laughing on the other side of his face.* He continued to Bruin: "Down to business; I'm going the extra mile for you, Bruin, just so you understand how fond I am of you. There's no one who'd work so tirelessly for you."

The bear thanked him, but thought that Reynard was dragging his feet.

"Now, uncle," said Reynard, "we'll need to go a fair distance. Follow me and I'll introduce you to as much honey as you can carry." The fox meant by this "as much honey as you can carry while being beaten," but the poor dimwit didn't spot the deeper meaning.

So they took themselves off to Lantfert's yard, where Bruin was deliriously happy.

Consider a moment this fellow Lantfert the carpenter. It was true what men said about him: he was a strong carpenter working with serious timber. Just the other day he'd brought a great oak into his yard, and begun to cut it. As carpenters do, he'd hammered two wedges in the oak, to force it open. Reynard was particularly happy to see the wedges, since they suited his plan perfectly. So he said to the bear, laughing all the while: "Just take a look at this tree; it's chockablock full of honey. See if you can get into it, but be careful not to eat too much! Honeycombs might be sweet and delicious, but take care not to eat too many. Eat them moderately, so you don't suffer indigestion. Dear uncle, it's me who'd get the blame if the honeycombs harmed you in any way."

"Cousin Reynard, don't be down in the mouth on my account! Do you take me for a fool? We should exercise moderation in all we eat."

"That's true; why should I be worried for you? Go as far as you can and creep into the tree."

Bruin the Bear rushed toward the honey, and stepped in with his two front feet, putting his head into the cleft of the tree. Reynard sprang lightly back and knocked a wedge out. At this point nothing could help Uncle Bruin, neither flattery nor reproach: he was stuck fast in the tree.

In this way the nephew brought his uncle into prison through trickery, so that the uncle couldn't escape at all. Brawn nor brain, foot nor head: nothing was going to help him.

Bruin's strength and courage were of no help at all. He saw that he was trapped, and began to roar and bray and scratch with his hind legs. He made such a racket that Lantfert the carpenter rushed out, knowing nothing of what this hullabaloo amounted to, carrying a sharp hook in his hand. Bruin remained fixed and frightened in the cleft of the tree, which held his head and forefeet fast. He twisted, he wrestled, and he roared, but it was no good: he was clueless about how to pull himself out.

From afar Reynard saw Lantfert the carpenter approaching. "How's the honey?" he asked Bruin. "Is it any good? Take care you don't overindulge, it won't do you any good. You won't be returning to court anytime soon once Lantfert comes. And try not to eat too much of what he'll dish out. I suggest you take a drink first, so it won't stick in your throat."

Having offered this advice, Reynard turned homeward to his castle. Lantfert came and found the bear stuck fast in the tree. He ran to his neighbors and said: "Come on, you lot, into my yard—there's a bear stuck fast there!"

Word spread instantly throughout the village. No one paused, but husbands and wives all ran as fast as they could, each armed either with staff, rake, or broom. Some pulled a stake from the hedge, some grabbed a flail. The priest picked up the cross, and the parish clerk brought a weather vane. The priest's wife Julocke came with her distaff—she'd been spinning.[10] Old women came, who had only single teeth left in their head.

Now Bruin wasn't feeling great: it was one against many. When he heard the villagers' terrific racket, he wrestled and pulled so hard that he extracted his head, but he left behind all the skin from his head and both his ears. No man ever saw a more hideous animal, for blood ran over his eyes. Before he could extract his feet, he had to leave his claws and paw pads behind.

The deal turned out badly for Bruin. He thought he'd never escape, now that his feet were so sore, and he couldn't see a thing because of the blood running down across his eyes. Lantfert approached with the priest. Everyone in the parish began to hit Bruin's head and face hard. He received plenty of hard knocks.

Every reader take note: if you're in a bad way, you're everyone's victim. The bear's story proves it: each of the villagers, great and small, were fierce and furious with him. Even old Hugelin with the crooked leg, and Ludolf with the broad, long nose—they were both ready to attack. One had a leaden hammer and the other a great leaden ball, and they let him have it with these. Then there were the villagers Sir Bertolt with the long fingers, Lantfert, and tall Ottram: these guys did more harm to the bear than all the others, since they had a sharp hook, and a crooked staff well leaded at the end, to play at ball. The villagers Baetkyn, Ende, Abelquak, my good Dame Bave, and the priest with his

10 In Catholic Europe, of course, priests were forbidden to marry. The picture of parish life given here falls far short of the doctrinal ideal.

No man ever saw a more hideous animal.

staff and Dame Julocke: they all inflicted so much harm on the bear that they would have happily killed him. They gave it to him with all they had.

Bruin the Bear sat and cried and groaned, for he had to take all that was dished out. Lantfert was the highest born of them all, and made the most noise, for Dame Pogge of Chafporte was his mother, and his father was Macob the stopper maker—a large, powerful, and independent type. They pelted Bruin with no shortage of stones. First Lantfert's brother sprang forward with a staff and whacked the bear on the head, so that he couldn't either hear or see.

The bear then sprang free between the bushes and the river among a crowd of women. He rushed with such force that he pushed a fair number of the villagers into the river, which was wide and deep. The priest's wife was among them, and he was so sorry to see his wife lying in the water that he left off beating the bear and cried, "Dame Julocke is in the water! Every man look to it! I'll absolve all the sins of those who can help!" Everyone then left Bruin the Bear and did as the priest asked.

When Bruin the Bear saw that they were running away from him to save the woman, he jumped into the water and swam as fast as he could. The priest shouted angrily and pursued the bear, crying, "Come back, you false thief!"

The bear swam into the fastest current and left them to their hue and cry. He was so glad to have escaped them. He bitterly cursed the honey tree, and the fox who'd betrayed him, since he'd crept in so far that he lost both cap and ears. It was two or three miles he swam downstream before he recovered from exhaustion on the bank. He was heavy of heart, groaning and sighing, with blood flowing into his eyes. He huffed and puffed as frantically as if he were dying.

And the fox? Before he returned from Lantfert's house he stole a plump hen and stuffed her in his pouch. He then ran smartly away on a path where he figured no one would come. Running in a sweat toward the river, he was beside himself with happiness, thinking the bear was dead. So he said to himself: "I have scored here, for now my biggest enemy in court is dead. And no one will blame me for his death! Why shouldn't I rejoice?"

With these words the fox looked toward the river, where he saw Bruin the Bear recovering. The moment he saw the bear, he was as depressed as he'd been happy before. He angrily told Lantfert off: "Damn you, Lantfert, you ignorant fool: may God give you a shameful death! You've lost such good meat that's rich and fat, and you've let the bear escape when you had him for the taking! Many's the man who'd have gladly eaten him. You've lost a fat bear!"

Blaming Lanfert in this way, he found the bear badly wounded by the river. Bruin was bloody and ill, for which he thanked no one so much as Reynard. Reynard scorned him: "Dear priest, *dieu vous garde*!"[11]

"Just look at the red thief," said the bear to himself; "I see the pitiless rascal coming."

"Haven't you forgotten something at Lantfert's?" said the fox. "I'm not sure you paid him for the honeycombs that you stole from him. If you haven't, it'd be disgracefully dishonest. I'd happily be the messenger myself to go and pay him. Wasn't the honey any good? I have more where that came from. Dear uncle, tell me, before I take off, what's the religious order you intend to enter? You're wearing a new hood. Is it a monk or an abbot

11 "May God protect you" (spoken by Reynard in French, the language of polite society, in order further to mock Bruin).

that you'll be? Whoever shaved your crown nipped off your ears. You seem to have lost your top, and removed your gloves. I'm inclined to think that you're off to sing compline."[12]

Bruin the Bear heard all this. He couldn't avenge himself, and this made him both furious and heavy-hearted. He let the fox say whatever he wanted to, and endured it with bitterness, before jumping back into the river. He was worried about his appearance in court, for he'd lost both ears, along with the skin and the claws of his forefeet.

If he'd been faced with a hunter wanting to kill him then and there, Bruin couldn't have escaped. Once he was out of the river he had to move, without knowing quite how to. So listen, then, to what he did: he sat upon his thighs and began to push himself forward on his hindquarters, painfully rolling and tumbling up to half a mile until he finally made it to court.

When they saw him from a distance, some in court were unsure what creature it was who rolled like that. Finally the King recognized him. You can be sure that he wasn't very pleased.

"This is Bruin the Bear, my friend. Lord God, who's wounded him? He's all red about the head! I'd say he's about to die. Where on earth can he have been?"

The beast came before the King and addressed him.

12 The final canonical hour of the day, a prayer spoken before going to bed.

9

The bear accuses the fox

"I lay a plaint to you, merciful lord Sir King, so you can see how I've been mistreated. I beg you to avenge this treatment on Reynard, the cruel beast. For I've been brutally handled in your service. I've lost both my front paws, along with my cheeks and my ears, by his treasonous deceit!"

"How dare that false thief Reynard do this!" replied the King. I declare, Bruin, and swear it by my crown, I'll avenge myself on him. You'll happily thank me, for sure."

The lion sent for all the wise beasts and demanded their counsel: How could he avenge the monstrous crimes of the fox?

The council concluded, old and young, that Reynard be summoned. He must be forced to suffer any sentence the court should give him. They judged Tybert the Cat best equipped to deliver the summons, because he was especially intelligent. The King thought this advice was good.

10

The King sends Tybert on another embassy to the fox. How Tybert fares with Reynard

"Sir Tybert," commanded the King, "go to Reynard, and deliver him a second summons: he must come to court to answer charges. Though he's cruel to other animals, he trusts you and will follow your advice. You'll tell him this. If he refuses to come, he'll receive a third summons. If he fails to come a third time, then we'll proceed mercilessly against him and all his family.

"My lord the King," replied Tybert, "those who counseled you weren't any friends of mine. What could I do there? Reynard won't come or go on my account. I beg you, dear King, send some other animal to him. I'm a small weakling. Bruin the Bear, who's so big and strong, couldn't bring him—how, then, should I do the job?"

"No," said the King, "Sir Tybert, you're wise and learned. Though you're small, there are a few crafty animals who can do more with brains than with brawn."

Tybert replied: "Someone has to it, so it might as well be me. God give me grace to succeed, for my heart is in my boots."

As Tybert was preparing to go directly to Wickedhole, he saw a St. Martin's bird come flying from a distance. He cried loudly: "Welcome, gentle bird, turn here and fly on my right side!"

The bird flew up to a tree that stood on the cat's left side. Tybert was uneasy—this was a bad omen, for had the bird flown on his right side, he would've been glad. Instead, he was full of foreboding that his journey wouldn't end well. He nonetheless did as many do, and gave himself better hope than his heart could muster.

So he ran toward Wickedhole. There he found the fox standing in front of his house. "God give you a good evening, Reynard. The King has threatened to execute you if you don't come to court with me right now."

"Tybert, my dear cousin, you're warmly welcome. May good fortune always be yours!"

It hurt the fox to speak kindly to the cat. Even if he uttered the words, his heart didn't think the same thing at all. We'll see that before they take their leave of each other.

"Let's spend the evening together," suggested Reynard. "I'll entertain you well, and tomorrow morning, first thing, we'll go together to court. Good nephew, let's act as I propose, since I've no kin whom I trust as well as I trust you. The traitor Bruin the Bear was here. He treated me so malevolently, and seemed so strong, that I wouldn't have accompanied him for a thousand pounds. But cousin, I'll go with you tomorrow morning early. First thing."

"It's best that we leave right now, for the moon is shining as brightly as if it were day. I never saw better weather."

"No, dear cousin, there are creatures who might meet us by day and treat us well. Those same creatures could mistreat us by night. To walk by night provokes suspicion. Therefore wait out this night here with me."

"What should we eat, if we stayed here?"

"There's nothing much to eat around here. You can have a good and sweet honeycomb. What do you say, Tybert—do you fancy some of that?"

"I don't care a farthing for honeycomb. Don't you have anything else? Now, if you were to give me a good fat mouse, I'd be better pleased."

"A fat mouse?" said Reynard. "Well, there's a priest living close by, with a barn by his house, in which there are so many mice that a cart couldn't carry them away. I've often heard the priest complain about the damage they do."

"Dear Cousin Reyner,[13] lead me there. I'll do anything for you in return."

"Sure, Tybert—but tell me the honest truth: Do you really love mice?"

"Love mice?" said the cat. "I love mice better than anything! Don't you know that mice taste better than venison, even than flans or pasties? If you want to do the right thing by me, take me to the mice! You'll win my love that way, even if you'd murdered both my parents and all my kin."

"You're pulling my leg."

"So help me God I'm not."

"Tybert," said the fox, "if I'd known that, I would've arranged for you to eat your fill of mice this very night!"

"My fill of mice?—that would be some haul!"

13 "Reyner" is an affectionate abbreviation of "Reynard," here used by Tybert to suggest (a false) intimacy between cat and fox.

"Really, Tybert, you're playing games with me."

"Not at all," he said. "If I had a fat mouse I wouldn't sell it for a gold coin."

"Let's go, then, Tybert. I'll bring you to the very place before we part."

"Reyner," said the cat, "with you as my guide, I'd happily go as far as Montpellier."[14]

So off they went together to the priest's barn. It was securely walled about with mud, which had been penetrated the night before by none other than the fox himself, who'd stolen a good fat hen from the priest. The angry priest had accordingly set a trap just in front of the hole to pay the fox back. He passionately wanted to capture him.

The fox, cunning thief that he was, knew all this well enough, and advised Tybert: "Cousin, creep into this hole, and you won't have to wait long before catching heaps of mice—can't you hear them squeaking already? I'll wait for you here at this hole until you return. Tomorrow we'll go to court together. So what's the holdup? Come on, so we can go back to my wife, who's waiting for us and will welcome us well."

"Cousin Reynard, let me get this straight: You're proposing that I go into this hole here? Priests are so wily and cunning. I'm afraid this will end badly."

"Fiddlesticks, Tybert! I never saw you afraid of anything. What's the matter with you, cat?"

The cat was ashamed and sprang directly into the hole, where

14 Montpellier (southern France) was famous in the Middle Ages for its university faculty of medicine.

he was instantly trapped by the neck before he could say "Jack Robin." Thus Reynard deceived his guest and cousin.

The moment Tybert was aware of the trap, he was afraid and tried to spring back out, but the trap had snapped shut. Tybert began to twist, as he was nearly strangled. He called out, wailing and making a hideous racket.

Reynard stood in front of the hole and heard it all. He was pleased with his trick, and said: "Tybert, you love mice as long as they are plump and good. If the priest or Martinet his son had known that, they're so kind they'd bring you a sauce to go with the mice. Tybert, you're singing while you eat. Is that how they act in court? Lord God, if Isengrim were stuck there with you, then I'd be really happy. He's afflicted me too often."

Tybert couldn't escape, but mewed and panted so loudly that Martinet, the priest's son, jumped up and cried out noisily: "God be thanked! My trap has caught the thief who's been stealing our hens. Everyone up! Payback time!"

With these words the priest got out of bed in a most unfortunate moment, and woke everyone else in the house.

He cried loudly: "The fox is taken!" Everyone leapt and ran. The priest himself ran out stark-naked. Martinet was the first to find Tybert. The priest gave an offering candle to Julocke, his wife, and asked her to light it at the fire, while he hit Tybert with a mighty staff. There were many hard strokes for Tybert across his whole body. Martinet was so angry that he knocked out one of the cat's eyes. The naked priest raised his staff and was about to strike when Tybert, seeing that he would certainly die, sprang between the priest's legs with claws spread and teeth bared, taking the priest's right stone with him. That leap shamed the priest.

The thing fell on the ground. When Dame Julocke saw it, she swore by her father's soul that she'd have rather paid a whole year's church-offering money than have the priest suffer this particular harm and shame. She said: "In the devil's name the trap was set there. Look, Martinet, dear son—this is your father's stone on the floor! I'm shamed and hurt, for even if he's healed of the wound, he's a man lost to me. He'll never be able to play that sweet game again!"

The fox stood on the outside of the hole and heard all this talk. He laughed so much that he could hardly stand. He spoke very quietly: "Dame Julocke, settle down and calm your sorrows. Even if the priest has lost one of his stones, it won't hinder his congress with you. There's many a chapel in this world in which only one bell is rung." Thus the fox scorned and mocked Dame Julocke the priest's wife, who was very upset.

The priest fell down in a swoon. They took him up and brought him to bed. The fox then returned to his territory, and left Tybert the Cat in great dread and danger. As far as the fox knew, the cat was as good as dead. But when Tybert saw that they were busy about the priest, he began to bite and gnaw right through the trap. He sprang out of the hole and went rolling and tumbling toward the King's court.

A beautiful dawn had broken before he arrived in court, in very sorry condition. He'd been poorly welcomed at the priest's house, and with the fox's advice his body had been beaten. Plus he was missing an eye.

When the King understood that Tybert had been treated in this way, he was plain furious. He uttered fierce threats against the thief Reynard, immediately summoning his council. He demanded to know how he might bring the fox to law.

Sir Grimbart, the fox's sister's son, spoke up: "Lords, even if my uncle were twice as bad, there is a remedy all the same. Let him be treated like a free man. He must be summoned a third time. If he still refuses to come, then he's guilty of all the crimes of which he's been accused."

"Grimbart," said the King, "who would you think should go and summon Reynard to come? Who will risk his ears, or his eye, or his life? Which animal has the courage? I don't believe there's anyone here foolish enough to do it."

Grimbart replied: "So help me God, I'm fool enough! I'll take the message to Reynard myself, if that's your command."

11

Grimbart the Badger brings Reynard to law, before the King himself

"ow off you go, Grimbart, and look out for yourself, for Reynard is dangerous, deceptive, and subtle. You'll need to look well about you and beware of him."

Grimbart said he would sort this matter out.

So Grimbart proceeded to Wickedhole. Went he arrived, he found Reynard the Fox at home. Dame Ermilyn his wife lay with her cubs in a dark corner.

Grimbart greeted his uncle and aunt: "Uncle, don't let absence from court damage you while you stand accused. If you think it wise, it's now high time that you accompanied me to court. Your continued absence can do you no good, since you're accused of many things there, and this is your third warning. I'm telling you the truth: if you hang around all day tomorrow, no mercy can help you—you'll see that within three days your house will be besieged. There'll be a gallows, and a rack erected in front of it. I'm telling you straight: You won't escape with either wife or child. The King shall take all your lives. So in my view it's best that you come with me to court. Your cunning will perhaps help you out of this tight spot. You've survived greater dangers before now, and who knows, you might be acquitted of each accusation, and all your enemies might be shamed. You've often wriggled out of tighter corners than what's required just now."

"What you say is true," replied Reynard. "The smart thing is for me to accompany you—now I'm all out of tricks. Perhaps the King will show mercy if I come to speak with him face-to-face. The court can't survive without me—the King understands that very well. Even if I have some enemies, it doesn't trouble me at all. All the council will judge me, but wherever great courts of kings or lords are gathered, Reynard must devise fine plans. Subtle stratagems are required. They can play their parts as much as they like, but mine is best, and I'll come out on top.

"There are many in court who've sworn to inflict maximum damage on me. This distresses me. For many hostile enemies are capable of more damage than one. All the same, nephew, it's better that I accompany you to court and answer for myself, rather than putting myself, my wife, and my children in danger of destruction. Come on, then, let's go. The King is more powerful than I am, so I have to do just as he wishes. Patiently suffering his will is the best I can do."

Reynard then spoke to Dame Ermilyn: "I put my cubs in your keeping. Look after them well, and especially Reynkin, my youngest son. He pleases me so well—I hope he'll follow in my steps. And there is Rosel, an exceptionally skillful thief. I love them as well as any man could love his children. If God protects me, I'll repay you properly when I return."

Thus Reynard took leave of his wife. God, how sorrowfully Ermilyn remained behind with the cubs! The supplier and caretaker of Wickedhole was gone, and the house wasn't stocked.

12

Reynard confesses himself

hen Reynard and Grimbart had traveled a certain distance together, Reynard said: "Dear cousin, I'm truly afraid, for I go in fear and danger of my life. I feel such repentance for my sins that I'll confess myself to you, dear cousin, since there's no priest available here. If all my sins were forgiven, my soul would be less troubled."

Grimbart answered: "Uncle, will you confess yourself? You must first promise to stop stealing and roving."

Reynard said that he well understood that. "Now hear, dear cousin, what I say: *Confiteor tibi, pater,*[15] of all the misdeeds that I've done. I'll gladly receive my penance for them."

Grimbart said: "What are you saying? Do you really wish to confess yourself? Then say it in English so that I can understand you!"

To which Reynard replied: "I've wronged all living animals, especially my Uncle Bruin the Bear, whose crown I made all bloody. And I taught Tybert the Cat to catch mice, for I taught her to leap into a trap where she was beaten. I also greatly wronged Chaunticleer and his children, of whom I've eaten a good many.

15 "I confess to you, father." Drawn from the prayer of confession in the mass of the Catholic Church.

"Uncle, will you confess yourself? You must promise first to stop stealing and roving."

"Neither has the King gone scot-free, since I've slandered him and the Queen so many times that they'll never wholly escape my wicked tongue.

"I've also tricked Isengrim the Wolf more times than I can count. I called him 'uncle,' for example, but that was only to deceive him, for he's no kin to me. I made him a monk at Elmare, where I myself also became one. That trick ended up hurting him and profiting me, for I had the bell rope tied to his feet. He so much enjoyed the ringing of the bell that he wished to learn how to do it, for which he ended up having good deal of grief. He rang so loudly that the folk in the street were afraid of the noise, and were puzzled as to what might be in the bell. They arrived before he had a chance to ask to be made a monk, and so he was beaten almost to death.

"After this I taught him to catch fish, and from those lessons he also ended up on the receiving end of many thumps.

"I also led him to the house of the richest priest in Vermedos. This priest had a pantry in which plenty of bacon was hanging. I'd been accustomed to filling my belly many times in this barn and had made a hole into which I made Isengrim creep. There he found the tubs with beef and many good cuts of bacon. But he ate so much and with such excessive gluttony that he wasn't able to get back out of the hole through which he'd entered, since his belly was so swollen.

"I went into the village and made a great racket, yet listen to what I did then: I ran to the priest where he sat eating as fat a capon as you could find anywhere. I grabbed that capon and ran away with it as fast as I could. The priest cried out and said, 'Take and kill that fox! I don't believe anyone ever saw anything so outrageous: the fox comes directly into my house and takes my hen from me right in front of my nose! Whoever saw a more shameless thief?'

"He took his table knife and threw it at me, but missed. I ran, and he shoved the table from him, in hot pursuit shouting, 'Kill him!' So I'm running fast, with all of them after me, and each wanting to harm me. I ran to exactly the place where Isengrim was, and there I let the capon drop, because it was too heavy for me. Against my will, I left it there, and then sprang through a hole where I wanted to be.

"As the priest picked up his capon, he saw Isengrim and cried, 'Hit him, friends! Here's the thief, the wolf—look to it that he doesn't escape!' They all ran together with sticks and staves, and made such a huge racket that all the neighbors came out and rained hard blows on him and threw big stones. He dropped as if he were dead. They dragged him and drew him across stones and stumps outside the village and threw him into a ditch, where he lay all night. I've no idea how he got out of that one.

"Afterward, on another occasion, Isengrim promised that he'd be my friend for a whole year after, if I'd help him fill his belly. So I led him to a place where I told him there were seven hens and a cock who sat on a perch. All were nice and fat. There was a trapdoor there, to which we climbed, at which point I told him to trust me: he need only creep through the door and he'd find many fat hens. Isengrim went laughing into the henhouse and tried to find hens here and there, finally saying to me, 'Reynard, you're pulling my leg, for I don't find what I'm looking for.'

" 'Dear uncle,' I said, 'if you creep in just a little farther, you'll find what you're after. If you want the prize, you need to take the risk! I've cleared the path for you.'

"So I made him creep yet farther in and shoved him so far

forward that he fell down on the floor, for the space was narrow. His fall was loud, at which all the sleepers sprang up. Those who slept beside the fire cried out that the trapdoor was open and that something had fallen in, but they had no idea what it was. They got up and lit a candle. When they saw Isengrim they struck and wounded him almost to death.

"Thus I've brought Isengrim into many tight corners—more than I can count. In fact I could remember many more if I put myself to it, which I'll tell you afterwards. I've also made love with Dame Arswind, his wife. I wish I hadn't, and I really regret this. It shamed her, and I'm truly sorry for it."

Grimbart said: "Uncle, I don't quite understand you. You say you've wronged his wife, but you speak as if you weren't being entirely sincere. I can't figure out what you mean, or where you've learned this kind of talk. Dear uncle, it'd be disgraceful if I openly confessed to having slept with my own aunt!"

"Nephew, I'm your uncle, and I'd upset you if I said anything against women. Now I've told you all that I can think of: give me my penance and absolve me, for I'm truly repentant."

Grimbart was subtle and wise. He snapped a branch off a tree and said: "Now, uncle, you'll hit yourself three times with this rod. Then lay it down on the ground and jump over it three times without bending your legs and without tripping over. Then pick it up and kiss it sweetly in token of your meekness and in obedience to your given penance, which I have imposed upon you. Herewith you are forgiven for all the sins you've committed up to today; I forgive them all."[16] The fox was delighted.

16 Grimbart takes on the role of priest (for which he has no authority whatsoever), and imposes a ridiculously easy penance, or punishment, for Reynard to perform.

Grimbart said to his uncle: "Uncle, look to it from now on that you do good works, read your psalms, go to church, observe feast days, make charitable gifts, and abandon your sinful and wicked life—your theft and your treason—so you'll deserve God's mercy." The fox duly promised that he'd do all this, and off they both went to court together.

Right by their route stood a cloister of black nuns, where many geese, hens, and capons walked outside the walls. As they went on talking, the fox led Grimbart out of the direct path, to where the poultry wandered outside the walls, just by the barn. The fox eyed them and noticed a nice fat young capon that sauntered along with his fellows. Reynard leapt on him and captured him. Feathers flew all over the place, but the capon escaped. Grimbart said: "Uncle, you cursed man, what are you up to? Will you fall again into your old ways for one of these capons? You've made a confession and you ought to be repentant!"

Reynard answered: "Truly, cousin, I forgot everything! Please pray to God to forgive me, for I'll never do it again."

Then they turned again to their road, and crossed a little bridge. The fox, all the while, kept a lookout for poultry, for he just couldn't help it. What sticks to the bone can't be cut away. Even if he were to be hanged, he'd be unable to stop looking out for poultry whenever he could see any.

Grimbart observed his manner and said: "False and deceptive fox! Just look at the way your eyes seek out poultry!"

The fox replied: "Cousin, you wrong me with such words. You're distracting me from my devotion and prayers. Let me say a Lord's Prayer for all the souls of poultry and geese that I've eaten and deceptively stolen from these holy nuns."

Grimbart wasn't too pleased, but the fox always kept his eye on the poultry, until at last they regained the main road. And then they took themselves to court. How Reynard trembled when they approached the court! He knew very well that he'd have to answer for the many serious felonies and robberies that he'd committed.

PART II

In a very tight corner, Reynard the Fox not only escapes hanging but turns the tables on all his enemies

13

Reynard comes to court and excuses himself before the King

At first, when it was known in court that Reynard the Fox and Grimbart his cousin had arrived, even those without kin and courtly supporters prepared to lay accusations on Reynard the Fox. Reynard conducted himself as if he hadn't a care in the world, and pretended to be in a much better position than he actually was. He passed proudly with his nephew through the main street of the city, looking as if he were the King's son and as if he hadn't wronged a soul in the slightest. He proceeded right through the main entrance of the court. Standing directly in front of the King, he said this:

"God grant you great honor and renown! Never did a King have a more faithful servant than I have been, and remain, to Your Grace. I nonetheless happen to know that there're many in this court who'd destroy me if only you'd believe them. Thanks be to God that it's beneath your crown lightly to believe these liars. We should complain to God Himself that these deceptive flatterers are most credited in lords' courts. These same villains are promoted so as to damage the good. The Lord God will duly pay them back for it!"

"Peace! Reynard, false thief and traitor!" said the King. "How well you can tell pretty stories, but they won't help you one jot. Do you think you can be my friend with such flattering words, you who have so often ill-served me, as we shall now know for sure? Have you observed the peace that I commanded?"

Chaunticleer couldn't contain himself, but crowed: "Think what I have lost in this peace!"

"Silence, Chaunticleer! Hold your tongue and let me do the talking to this foul thief!

"You robber, you say you love me, and that you've treated my messengers well—those poor fellows Tybert the Cat and Bruin the Bear, who are both still bloody. Don't deny it or speak up for yourself—it'll cost you your life this very day!"

"In the name of the Father and Christ the son,"[17] said the fox, "dear lord and mighty King: if Bruin's crown is bloody, what's that to do with me? He was the one who ate honey at Lantfert's house in the village, and brought the harm on himself, when he was beaten. If he'd wanted to, he could have taken vengeance—he's such a strong fellow—before he jumped in the water. Then Tybert the Cat came, whom I welcomed politely. If he went out without my advice to steal mice at a priest's house and the priest punished him, should I be blamed? If so, I wouldn't be happy, my liege lord. You can do what you will with me, regardless of the justice of my cause. You can boil, roast, hang, or blind me: I'm unable to escape you, and we all stand under your jurisdiction. You're mighty and strong, while I am feeble, with no resources if you put me to death. You wouldn't need much to take vengeance on me."

17 The beginning of a Trinitarian liturgical formula.

While they were speaking, Bellin the Ram and his ewe Oleway sprang up. "My lord the King, hear our accusation!"

Bruin the Bear stood up, with all his family and supporters. The whole crowd was there: Tybert the Cat, Isengrim the Wolf, Cuwaert the Hare, the panther and the boar, the sheep, Brunel the Goose, the kid and the goat, Boudewyn the Ass, Bore the Bull, Hamel the Ox, the weasel, along with Chaunticleer the Cock and Pertilote and all their offspring. The whole lot of them made a huge uproar. They came openly in front of the King, and forced the arrest of the fox.

14

Reynard is arrested and condemned to death

he King convened a parliament to address the matter of Reynard's offenses. It was judged that he should be put to death. The fox answered all the charges. No one ever heard charges so well put from such beasts, nor, from the other side, such subtle defensive inventions. The fox defended himself so brilliantly, and with such technical skill, that those who heard him were amazed. Those who heard and saw it can tell the whole truth about it, so I'll be brief and focus on the fox.

The King and the council heard witnesses for the prosecution with regard to Reynard's transgressions. It ended up going with them as it often does: the weakest had the worst of it.

They delivered their judicial sentence: that the fox should be put to death, hanged by the neck. At this news Reynard didn't feel so playful. All his flattery and deception were useless to him now. The judgment was delivered and couldn't be avoided. Grimbart his nephew and many of his extended family didn't have the heart to watch him die, and so took their leave of the court.

The King considered the matter and noticed how many of his young subjects, who were closely related to Reynard, left weeping. He said this to himself: "Here I need to think again. Reynard is certainly a felon, but there're many good men in his family."

Tybert the Cat spoke: "Sir Bruin and Sir Isengrim: How slow you are! It's almost evening. There are plenty of hedges and bushes hereabouts, and if he escaped from us and were delivered from this danger, he'd never be captured again. He's so wily and subtle, and he knows so many tricks! So will we hang him or not? Why are you all standing around—it'll be nighttime before the gallows will be ready!"

Isengrim considered the matter: "There's a gallows right beside us."

But he sighed as he spoke. The cat noticed this and said: "Isengrim—you're afraid! Is this being done against your will? Don't you remember that Reynard worked hard to put both your brothers to death by hanging? If you had any brains, you'd repay him, and not delay so long."

15

Reynard is led to the gallows

Isengrim was taken aback: "You're making too much of a fuss, Sir Tybert. If we had a good halter fit for his neck and it were strong enough, we'd soon put paid to the fox."

Reynard, who hadn't said anything for some while, addressed Isengrim: "Shorten my agony. Tybert owns a strong cord that caught him in the priest's house when he bit the priest's stone off. He can climb well and moves quickly—let him pull on the rope. Isengrim and Bruin: it's right that you should treat your nephew in this way. I'm sorry that I live so long! Get on with the job—it's a sorry business that you're being so slow about it. Go on ahead, Bruin, and lead me away. Isengrim: you follow us, and be on the lookout that I don't escape."

Bruin the Bear remarked: "What Reynard says is the best advice I've ever heard."

So Isengrim immediately commanded his kin and friends to be certain that Reynard didn't escape, for, he said, "He's wily and deceptive." They held him both by the feet and by the beard, so ensuring that he didn't give them the slip.

The fox heard all these words that concerned him so directly,

"Get on with the job—it's a sorry business that you're being so slow about it."

yet said this: "Dear Uncle Isengrim, I feel you're going to too much trouble to inflict pain and damage on me. If I were so bold, I'd beg you to be merciful, even though my pain and sorrow is welcome to you. I well know that if my aunt your wife remembered old times, she wouldn't permit harm of any kind to me. I'm wholly at your mercy to do with me now whatever you like. May God give you, Bruin and Tybert, a horrible death if you don't inflict on me the worst you can. I know where I'm going—one dies but once. In fact I wish I were already dead! I saw my father die, and it was all over quickly."

"Let's get to it!" said Isengrim. "You're blaming us for working too long, so let's not delay a second longer!"

He advanced aggressively on one side, while Bruin stood on the other, and so led Reynard to the gallows. Tybert, whose throat was still sore from the trap, and whose gullet still hurt from blows delivered through the trickery of the fox, capered ahead of them and carried the rope, thinking that he was finally about to get even.

Tybert, Isengrim, and Bruin went rapidly with Reynard to the appointed place where felons were executed. Noble the King, the Queen, and all the courtiers followed to watch Reynard's death. The fox was afraid lest matters went south, and thought rapidly about how he could escape death. He also thought about how he could trick and shame those three who wished him dead, by deceiving the King to come over to his side against them. He thought only about this—how he could escape with trickery.

This is what he thought: *It's no surprise that the King and many others are angry with me—I deserve it, though I still hope to be their best friend. And yet I'll never do a good turn for one of them! I don't care how strong the King is, or how wise his councils. As long as I can speak, I'll rise as high in court as they would have me on the gallows. I've got so many tricks up my sleeve!*

Then Isengrim said: "Sir Bruin, think about your red head, which you got through Reynard's tricks. Now we can pay him back fair and square. Tybert: you weigh the least. Climb up quickly and bind the rope tightly to the beam. Make a slip knot or a noose. You'll get your revenge on him today. Bruin, look to it that Reynard doesn't escape—hold him tight! I'll help set up the ladder, so he can mount it."

Bruin said: "Trust me! I'll hold him well!"

The fox then said: "Now I'm really scared, because I see death coming my way and I can't escape. My lord the King, and dear Queen, and all of you who stand by: I ask but one concession before I take my leave of this world, that I might be allowed to make my confession openly and recount my sins so clearly that my soul isn't burdened. I don't want anyone to be blamed afterwards for my robberies, or for my treason. My death will be more acceptable to me, and I ask that you each pray to God that He have mercy on my soul."

16

Reynard makes open confession in the presence of the King and of all those who would hear it

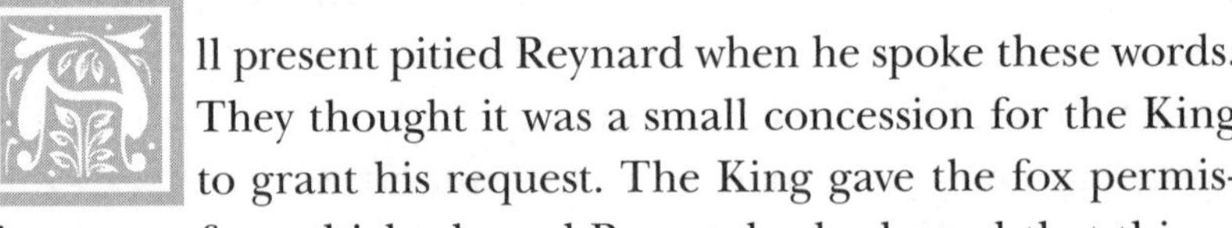

All present pitied Reynard when he spoke these words. They thought it was a small concession for the King to grant his request. The King gave the fox permission to confess, which pleased Reynard, who hoped that things might yet take a turn for the better.

This is what he said: "Now God help me! I have wronged everyone here. I was, nonetheless, one of the best children anywhere since the moment I was weaned. I went and played with the lambs because I gladly heard them bleat. I spent so much time with them that I bit one, and so first learned to lap blood, which tasted so good. After I got a taste for flesh, I hungered after more. So I went with the goats into the forest where I heard the kids bleat, and I killed a couple of them. I grew courageous once I'd killed hens and geese wherever I found them. My teeth became completely bloody after this. I became so fierce and angry that I killed whatever I could catch.

"I then happened to find Isengrim in winter, where he hid under a tree. He told me that he was my uncle. When I heard him relate our family connection, we teamed up, which I now wish had not happened. We swore to each other to be faithful and to hold fast together, and began to roam as a pair. He stole the big things and I the small. Everything was common property between us, even if he had the best deal and I didn't get even half of mine. Whenever Isengrim got a calf or a sheep, he looked fierce and angrily drove me away, keeping both his part and mine. He's such a good guy, is Isengrim!

"Yet these affairs were trifling. Whenever we had the luck to take an ox or a cow, Isengrim turned up with his wife and seven children, so that not even the smallest ribs came my way: they'd eat up all the flesh, and I had to be content with my lot, given that I didn't need it quite as much as they did. For I've got so much treasure, both silver and gold, that seven carts wouldn't be able to carry it."

When the King heard Reynard speak of this treasure of his, he burned with greedy desire for it.

"Reynard, might you tell me what's happened to all this treasure?"

The fox replied: "My lord, I'll tell you the whole story. The treasure was stolen. If it hadn't been stolen, it would have cost you your life: you would have been murdered, heaven forbid, which would have been the most dreadful event under heaven."

When the Queen heard this she took fright and cried loudly: "Oh, dear, Reynard: What are you saying? I beg you in the name of the long voyage which your soul is about to make, tell us the plain truth of what you know about the murder that was planned for my lord. Speak so we can all hear it now!"

Listen to the way in which the fox flatters the King and the Queen, and how he wins their goodwill and love. Listen also to how he blocks those who work for his death. He'll unpack his bag of tricks by flattery, and lie with seductive words. He'll make it seem as if everything he said should be taken as gospel truth.

With a mournful expression the fox addressed the Queen: "Now I can't escape death. Given that you beg me so passionately, I'm unprepared to endanger my soul. If I did, I'd be going into the eternal pains of hell. I won't say a thing that I can't prove, for the King would have been horribly murdered by members of his own court. I have to say that those who were most involved in this conspiracy were my next of kin, whom I'd not betray, were it not for the pains of hell threatening me."

The King was somber. "Reynard, are you telling me the truth?"

"I'm afraid so," said the fox. "Don't you see my predicament? Would I damn my soul? What would I gain by telling anything but the truth? I'm on the very brink of death: neither prayer nor wealth can help me."

Then the fox trembled deceitfully, as if he were afraid. The Queen pitied him, and begged the King to treat him mercifully so as to avoid any more damage, and to command the people to hold their peace and give audience to the fox.

The King commanded everyone to hold their tongue and permit the fox to say whatever he wanted, without let or hindrance. So listen to what he said.

"So," said the fox, "now that you are all still, and since it's the King's will, I'll openly declare this treason. As I do, I'll not spare anyone whom I know to be guilty."

17

Reynard endangers all who wished to execute him, and secures the King's grace

ow observe how the fox began. He called Grimbart, his dear cousin, who'd always helped him in a tight spot, as a witness. He did so because Grimbart's testimony would be more credible, and so he could lie more persuasively about his enemies.

So he began: "My lord and father had found King Ermeric's treasure buried in a pit. When he took possession of this treasure, he grew proud and arrogant to the point that he held all other animals, who'd previously been his companions, in low esteem. He sent Tybert the Cat into the wild territory of Ardennes to Bruin the Bear,[18] to pay homage to Bruin. He ordered Tybert to tell Bruin that if he wanted to be King, he should come to Flanders. Bruin was delighted by this news, because he'd long wished to be King. So Bruin went to Flanders, where my father received him graciously. He immediately sent for my nephew the wise Grimbart, along with Isengrim the Wolf and Tybert the Cat. These five then met up between Ghent and the village of Ifte. There they plotted together a whole long, dark night. With the

18 The Ardennes Forest, in modern Belgium and Luxembourg.

devil's help and skill, and with my father's wealth, they conspired and swore to the King's death.

"Now listen to the astonishing business: the four of them swore on Isengrim's head that they'd make Bruin King and lord, and bring him to the throne at Aachen,[19] where they'd set the crown on his head. If there were any of the King's friends or kin who resisted, then my father would, with all his wealth, drive them out and deprive them of their power.

"One morning it chanced that Nephew Grimbart, drunk with wine, revealed the plot in secrecy to his wife Sloepcade, and told her to keep it secret. She immediately forgot her oath and confessed it to my wife, on a heath where they had both gone on pilgrimage. She confessed it only as long as my wife first swore on her honor and by the three holy Kings of Cologne that she would never, for love or hate, tell it to another soul but keep it secret. My wife, however, didn't keep it secret at all when she got home to me. She revealed all she'd heard, as long as I'd keep it all secret. She supplied so many tokens of evidence that I judged it was true. My hair stood on end and my heart grew heavy as lead and as cold as ice.

"I remembered that a similar thing happened to the frogs a while ago.[20] The frogs were free, and yet complained that they had no King and weren't governed, since a community without a

19 Aachen (French Aix-la-Chapelle), in Western Germany, near Cologne. Aachen was an imperial city of Charlemagne (ca. 742-814) and the place where German kings preferred to be crowned, between the tenth and fifteenth centuries.

20 An Aesopian fable, translated by Caxton in his own volume of Aesopian materials. See William Caxton, *Caxton's Aesop*, ed. R. T. Lenaghan (Harvard: Harvard University Press, 1967), pp. 90-91, for Caxton's own version of this fable.

governor was undesirable. So they appealed loudly to God that He'd ordain one to rule over them: they all desired this. God heard their request. Because it was not unreasonable, He sent a stork, who swallowed as many of them as he could find. He was utterly pitiless. The frogs complained, but by then it was too late: those who were previously free and afraid of no one were now bound and obliged to strengthen their King. For this reason, rich and poor, I feared that the same might happen to us.

"Thus, my lord King, I was so worried about you, for which you're repaying me now with small thanks. I know Bruin the Bear is a vicious, rapacious thief. I thought that if he were King we'd all be destroyed. I also know that our sovereign lord the King is a figure of such high birth—so mighty and so generous and so merciful—that I thought a change involving acceptance of a stinking thief, and repudiation of a noble, mighty, stately lion, would have been truly disastrous. For the bear and his ancestors have more mad craziness in their dumb heads than anyone else. So I was really sorry and thought hard about how I could obstruct and break my father's treacherous counsel, which was set to make a lord and King of a peasant traitor who was worse than a thief.

"I prayed continually to God, that He'd preserve our King in honor and health, and grant him long life. But I also thought that if my father should keep his treasure, he'd manage to find a way to depose the King.

"I was hard-pressed to think where my father had hidden his treasure. I spied as closely as I could at all times in woods, bushes and fields where my father seemed to be checking things. Whether it was by night or day, in cold weather or hot, I was always beside him to work out where his treasure was laid up.

"Once I lay down flat on the ground and saw my father running out of a hole. Now listen to what I saw him do: When he came out of the hole he looked quickly about him to discover if he'd been seen. When he couldn't see anyone, he stopped up the hole with sand and made it even and plain like the ground around it. He had no idea that I'd seen this. He stroked the ground where his tracks were with his tail, and licked the ground so that no one would notice the tracks. I learned tricks then from my father that I'd never known about before. He then left and went off to the village on business.

"I wasn't slow about it, but leapt to the hole. No matter how well he supposed that he'd secured it, I wasn't such a fool that I couldn't easily find the hole. I scratched and scraped at the sand with my feet and crept in, where I found a bigger pile of silver and gold than I'd ever seen. There is no one here who's ever seen so much in a single heap in all his life. I then took Ermilyn my wife to help me and we didn't rest by day or night before we'd carried away this precious treasure with immense labor to another place, situated much better under a hedge in a deep hole.

"While my wife and I were working away, my father was with those who were conspiring against the King. Now hear what they did. Bruin the Bear and Isengrim sent word to all the surrounding territory declaring that, if any man wanted wages, he should come to Bruin and he'd pay them. My father ran through the land bearing the letters, not having a clue that he'd been robbed of his treasure. For all the world, he'd not find a penny of it.

"When my father had moved across all the territory between the Elbe and the Somme, and had hired plenty of soldiers to supply Bruin the following summer, he returned to the bear and his fellows. He reported to them his adventures in the land of Saxony—how hunters and their hounds had pursued him every day, and how he'd barely escaped alive. After telling them all this, he showed the four traitors some letters. These hugely pleased Bruin, since the names of twelve of Isengrim's family were written in them, not counting the bears, the foxes, the cats and the badgers, who had all sworn to stand ready when the first messenger should call them to help the bear, as long as they had their wages a month in advance. Thank God I saw all this!

"After his report, my father went to the treasure hole to gaze on the hoard. Now he began to suffer grievously, once he failed to find what he was looking for, since his hole had been broken and the treasure carried off. The way he acted then makes me weep: in anger and sorrow he went and hanged himself.

"Thus stood Bruin's conspiracy, because of my cunning. Now consider my bad lot: the traitors Isengrim and Bruin were in the King's innermost circle, and sat with him on the high bench of justice, whereas I, poor Reynard, had no thanks or reward. I buried my own father so the King should live.

"My lord," said the fox, "where are they who'd act in this way—that's to say, who'd destroy themselves to save you?"

The King and the Queen hoped to win the treasure. Without taking counsel, they brought Reynard into their confidence, asking him if he'd be so kind as to tell them where the treasure was.

"How," Reynard replied, "should I tell the King, or those who'd hang me to protect the traitors and murderers, where my treasure is? With their flattery they want only to kill me. I'd be crazy to do that!"

The Queen then spoke: "Not at all, Reynard, the King grants you your life, and pardons you completely as long as you're a wise and faithful counselor to my lord."

"Dear lady, if the King believes me and if he will pardon and forgive all my past crimes, then there will never be so rich a King as I'll make him, with the precious and incalculable treasure that I'll put in his possession."

The King answered: "Ah, my lady, will you believe the fox? I don't mean to offend you, but he's born to rob, steal, and lie. Treachery is innate to him—it cleaves to his very bones and can't be drawn out of him."

"No, my lord, you can believe him this time, even though he was a felon in the past. Now he's a changed man: you've heard him indict his father and his nephew the badger. He would've accused other beasts if he'd been a false and treacherous liar."

The King said: "My lady, if you see it like that, and think it best to act in this way, I'll take responsibility for all the crimes of Reynard and believe him, even though it might end up harming me. But I swear by my crown that if he breaks the law just one more time, he and his family will pay for it unto the ninth degree!"

The fox looked on the King from time to time, and was secretly glad. "I'd be stupid not to tell the whole truth," he said.

The King picked up a straw from the ground, and proceeded to pardon the fox for all his and his father's crimes. No wonder the fox was happy, for he was no longer in danger of death, and had got off scot-free from the power of his enemies.

"My lord the King, and my noble lady the Queen: God repay the great honor you do me! I'll think how I can best thank you for it, so that you'll be the richest King in the world. There's no one alive to whom my treasure is better entrusted than to you both."

Then the fox picked up a straw, and gave it to the King, saying: "My most dear lord, may it please you to receive here the rich treasure that King Ermeric once had, for I give it to you with a liberal heart and acknowledge it openly."

The King received the straw and tossed it jokingly aside with a laugh, thanking the fox profusely. The fox laughed to himself.

The King carefully listened to the fox's counsel. All those present stood entirely at his disposition. "My lord," he said, "now listen, and mark my words well. To the west of Flanders there's a forest called Hulsterloe, and a lake called Krekenpit nearby. This area is so deserted that sometimes no one goes there in a whole year except those who know what they're about. That's where the treasure lies hidden. Note that the place is called Krekenpit. I would advise you, so as to avoid any harm whatsoever, that you and my lady go there together. I don't know anyone trustworthy enough whom I'd trust to go in your stead. So go yourself.

"When you come to Krekenpit, you'll find two birch trees right beside the pit. My lord, go to the birch trees: that's where the buried treasure is. You'll have to scrape and dig a little moss away from one side. You'll find many jewels set in gold and silver. You'll also find the crown that King Ermeric wore in his time—the one Bruin the Bear would've worn if he'd had his way. You'll see many expensive jewels, with precious stones set in gold, which cost thousands of pounds. When, my lord the King, you've taken possession of all this treasure, how often will you say in your heart: *Reynard, Reynard—how trustworthy you were after all, you who through your subtlety buried and hid this treasure trove here! May God grant you good chance wherever you are right now!*"

The King replied: "Sir Reynard, you must join us in digging up this treasure: I don't know the way, and won't ever be able to find it. I've often heard of Paris, London, Aachen, and Cologne.

But it strikes me that you are playing with us, since the place name Krekenpit is made-up."

This order wasn't good for the fox, who, dissembling, replied indignantly: "My lord the King, you're as close to the truth as Rome is from the moon. Do you imagine that I'd lead you up the garden path? Never! I'll dispel your doubts and direct you to the place with good testimony."

He called loudly: "Cuwaert the Hare, up you come before the King!" The beasts looked to the King and wondered what he would do.

The fox said to the hare: "Cuwaert, are you cold? Why all the trembling and shaking? No need to be afraid, but tell my lord the King the truth. I charge you to do so by the faith and loyalty you owe both him and my lady the Queen in all such matters as I'll require of you."

Cuwaert replied that he'd tell the truth even if he'd lose his life in telling it. "I won't lie, if I know the truth—you've ordered me so forcefully."

"Then tell us: Don't you know where Krekenpit is?"

The hare said: "I knew twelve years ago very well where Krekenpit was—why ask me this question? It's in a forest called Hulsterloe in a warren in the wilderness.

"I've endured hunger and cold there, more than I can tell. That's where Father Simonet the Frisian[21] used to counterfeit money, which he used to support himself and all his associates. But that was all before I became friends with Ryn the Dog, who helped me escape many dangers, as he could well testify if he

21 Frisia extends along the northwest coast of the Netherlands and along the coasts of both Germany and Denmark.

were here. Never in my days did I wrong the King or do otherwise than I should have done within the law."

Reynard replied: "Return to that company, Cuwaert, now that my lord the King is not interested in hearing anything more from you." The hare returned and went again to the place from which he'd come.

The fox said: "My lord the King: Is what I said proven true?"

"Yes, Reynard," said the King. "Forgive me. I was wrong not to believe you. Now, dear Reynard, lead us the way to the pit where the treasure is."

The fox replied: "It's amazing. Can you really believe that I wouldn't go with you if I could? If it were in any way possible for me to come with you, as long as it caused no embarrassment to Your Lordship, I'd come for sure. But I'm afraid it's just not possible. Listen to what I must say, even though it disgraces and shames me to do so.

"When Isengrim the Wolf, in the devil's name, entered a religious order and became a shaven monk, the food for six monks wasn't enough for him. He complained and lamented so insistently that I pitied him as my kinsman, because he'd grown lethargic and ill. I counseled him to abandon his religious vocation, which is exactly what he did.

"I therefore stand cursed by the Pope's ban and judgment. So I intend to travel to Rome first thing tomorrow to be forgiven and pardoned for this.[22] From Rome I'll go by sea to the Holy Land and will never return until I've done so many good works that I can accompany you honorably. My lord the King, it'd bring

22 Rome was one of the principal destinations for pilgrims seeking pardon for sin.

you disgrace if I were to join you now in any land. It'd be said that you traveled with a person under sentence."

The King replied: "Since the Church has censured you, it would be judged beneath my dignity if you accompanied me. I'll therefore take Cuwaert or someone else to show me Krekenpit. I advise you, Reynard: absolve yourself from the Pope's judgment."

"My lord the King," said the fox, "I'll go to Rome as quickly as I can, just as you say. I won't rest by night or day until I've been forgiven."

"Reynard, it strikes me that you are converted to the right path. God give you grace to accomplish your spiritual goal!"

As soon as this discussion ended, the noble King went and stood on a raised stage of stone. He commanded silence to all the beasts. They were all to sit in a ring around him on the grass, according to rank and birth. Reynard the Fox stood by the Queen, whom he had reason to love well.

The King then declared: "Hear ye, all who are poor and rich, young and old, who are present here before me. Reynard, one the principal officers of my household, had acted so badly that he was to have been hanged this very day. He has now, in this court, done so much that my wife the Queen and I have promised him our grace and friendship. The Queen has pleaded so actively for Reynard that I have made my peace with him. I freely give him his life and limbs.

"I further command, on pain of death, that you respect Reynard, his wife, and his children, wherever you should happen to meet them, by day or night. I'll hear no more accusations against Reynard. If he's committed crimes before now, he will no more. He will instead mend his ways. Tomorrow morning he's off early to the Pope for pardon and forgiveness for all his sins."

Tiselin the Raven heard this pronouncement, and leapt to where Isengrim, Bruin, and Tybert were sitting: "How do you think you're going now? You're in for it. You poor saps, what are you doing here? Reynard is now a squire, honored and mighty in the court. The King has judged him free of all charges and has forgiven him his misdeeds. Each of you will be betrayed and indicted."

Isengrim said, "How can this be? I think you're lying, Tiselin."

"Not so."

The wolf and the bear then went to the King. Tybert the Cat was deeply distressed because he was so afraid. To have the friendship of the fox he'd forgive the loss of his eye at the priest's house. He was so upset that he had no idea what to do. He wished he'd never seen the fox, and left court.

18

The wolf and the bear are arrested through the work of Reynard the Fox

Isengrim walked arrogantly across the court and stood in front of the King. He thanked the Queen and angrily spoke ill of the fox, so that the King heard it. The King himself was angered by this, and ordered the immediate arrest of the wolf and the bear. Never was more harm done to mad dogs than was done to them. They were both so tightly bound all night that they could stir neither hand nor foot. They were scarcely able to roar or move a single limb.

Now listen to how the fox worked. He hated the bear and the wolf, and persuaded the Queen to grant him this: as much as a foot length and width of the bear's skin from his back, to make a pilgrim's pouch for himself.

The fox was then ready, except that he needed four sturdy shoes. So listen to how he got those shoes. He said to the Queen: "Madam, I'm your pilgrim. Here's my Uncle Sir Isengrim, who has four strong shoes that would serve me well. If he would give me just two of them, I'd actively pray for your soul's health on my pilgrimage. For it's right and proper that a pilgrim always think of and pray for those who support him. And you'd profit your soul, if you want to, if you could also procure two shoes from my Aunt Arswind. She can spare them easily, because she goes about only rarely, and stays always at home."

The Queen then said: "Reynard, it's only fitting that you have shoes such as these. You can't very well do without them. They'll serve to keep your feet in good state as you cross many a high mountain and many stony roads. You couldn't find a better set of shoes than those of Isengrim and his wife, since they're good and strong. Even if it endangers their life, each of them shall give you two shoes for you to perform your noble pilgrimage."

19

Isengrim and his wife Arswind are obliged to have their shoes plucked off. Reynard puts the shoes on to go to Rome

So the false pilgrim has his two shoes from Isengrim's feet. They were pulled off from the claws to the sinews. Never did you see a hen being roasted who lay more still than did Isengrim when his shoes were pulled off. He didn't move a muscle, even though his feet bled when he was unshod. Then his wife Dame Arswind was required to lie down in the grass in somber mood. In addition, she lost her two hind shoes.

The fox was overjoyed, and spoke scornfully to his aunt: "My dear aunt, it pains me that you've suffered so much for me, except in this one respect: you're the dearest of all my kin, and so I'll gladly wear your shoes. You'll also profit from my pilgrimage, and share in the pardon that I will, with the help of your shoes, fetch from across the sea."

Dame Arswind was so angry that she could hardly speak a word. She nonetheless said this: "Ah, Reynard, now you have all you want. I hope God avenges it!"

Isengrim and his companion the bear held their peace, since

they were ill at ease, for they were tied up and sorely wounded. Had Tybert the Cat been there, he would have suffered too. He wouldn't have escaped without some distress and shame.

The next day, when the sun was up, Reynard had the shoes that he'd taken from Isengrim and Arswind greased. He donned them and went to the King and Queen, speaking happily to them: "Noble lord and lady, God give you a good day! I desire of Your Grace that a priest bless my pilgrim's bag and staff. That's only right and proper for a pilgrim."

The King then sent for Bellin the Ram. When he came, the King said: "Sir Bellin, you'll say a mass for Reynard and give him his pouch and staff, because he's about to go on pilgrimage."

The ram replied: "I daren't do that, for Reynard has said that he's been cursed by the Pope."

"What of that?" said the King. "Master Gelys has explained to us that no matter how much a man has sinned, as long as he intends to forsake those sins, confess himself, and receive penance and make satisfaction by the priest's counsel, then God will forgive him and be merciful. Reynard will travel abroad to the Holy Land to be forgiven all his sins."[23]

Bellin answered the King: "I refuse to get involved in this matter in any way, unless you protect me from harm in the spiritual court before Bishop Take-it-now and before his Archdeacon Loose-wind, and before his official Sir Lets-take-it-all."

The King started to get angry and said: "I won't ask you this much for a long while. I'd prefer to hang you than be forced to ask you so insistently."

When the ram saw that the King was angry, he was so afraid

23 Jerusalem was also an especially important pilgrimage site.

that he trembled. He went straight to the altar and sang from his books and read those things that seemed appropriate to Reynard, who didn't much care for any of it, except that the blessing would make him look good.

After Bellin the Ram had performed all this service devoutly, he hung a pouch, covered with the skin of Bruin the Bear, on the fox's neck, along with a small prayer book. Reynard was ready for his journey. He turned to the King as if he were sad to leave, and pretended to weep as if he were grieving in his heart. If he had any sorrow whatsoever, however, it was only because all the others weren't trapped in the same way he'd caught the wolf and the bear. All the same, he stood and asked all of them to pray for him, just as he would pray for them.

The fox thought he was tarrying too much, and would gladly have left, since he knew perfectly well he was guilty. The King said: "Reynard, it pains me that you're so impatient to leave and won't stay any longer."

"No, my lord, it's time to go, for one shouldn't waste time in doing good works. I pray you give me leave to depart, for I must perform my pilgrimage."

"God be with you now," said the King. And he commanded the entire court to accompany Reynard on his way, except the wolf and the bear, both of whom lay bound. No one dared show any sign of pity for them. And if only you could have seen Reynard—how meekly he went forth with his pouch and his Psalter on his shoulder and his shoes on his feet! You'd have laughed.

He started out, putting on a wise face to the world. In his heart, however, he was amused by the fact that all those who accompanied him had, only a little time earlier, been so hostile to him. And he now judged the King, who'd hated him so intensely, in the same way. Reynard had made such a fool of him and had fully satisfied his objective. He was now a humble pilgrim.

"My lord the King," said the fox, "I pray you to return now. I wouldn't want you to come any farther with me, since harm might befall you if you did. You've arrested two murderers. If they escaped, you might be harmed by them. I pray that God keep you from misadventure."

With these words he stood on his hind legs, and asked all the animals, great and small, who wished to share in his pardon that they should pray for him. They all said that they'd remember him in their prayers.

Reynard parted from the King and his court with such sadness that many of them felt sad themselves. He then said happily to Cuwaert the Hare and Bellin the Ram: "Dear friends, shall we take our leave of each other already? You and God will accompany me farther. Neither of you ever made me angry. You're good to walk with—you're courteous, friendly, and no beast ever laid an accusation against you. You're of good character, and holy in your living. You both live as I did when I was a recluse. As long as you have leaves and grass you're happy. You don't care about bread, flesh, or any food of that kind." With such flattering words Reynard seduced these two.

They accompanied him until they came to his house at Wickedhole.

PART III

Reynard the Fox mocks the stupidity of the lion's court

20

Cuwaert the Hare is slain by the fox

When the fox came to the gate of his house, he told Bellin the Ram: "Cousin, you'll wait outside here. Cuwaert and I will go in. I'll ask Cuwaert to help me take my leave of Ermilyn my wife, and to comfort her and my children."

Bellin replied: "I pray that he give them good comfort."

With such flattering words he brought the hare into his hole. It would be an evil hour for the hare. There they found Dame Ermilyn lying on the ground with her young, who had been very distressed at the prospect of Reynard's death. When she saw him enter she was glad, though when she noticed the pouch, the prayer book, and the shoes, she was amazed and said: "My dear Reynard, how did you get on?"

"I was arrested in court, but the King released me. Now I have to go on pilgrimage. Bruin the Bear and Isengrim the Wolf are standing bail for me. I'm grateful to the King for giving us Cuwaert here to do whatever we want with. The King himself said that Cuwaert was the first to lay an accusation against us. And by the trust I owe to you, in fact, I'm extremely angry with Cuwaert."

When Cuwaert heard these words he was plain frightened. He wanted to flee but couldn't, because the fox stood between him and the door. Reynard caught him by the neck. Then the hare cried: "Help, Bellin! Where are you? This pilgrim is killing me."

But that cry was soon ended, because the fox bit his throat in two. Then he said: "Let's go eat this good fat hare." The young cubs came up too. So they held a great feast, because Cuwaert had such a good fat body. Ermilyn ate the flesh and drank the blood. She repeatedly thanked the King that he'd made them so merry.

"Eat as much as you want," said the fox; "the King will pay for it, as long as we do the fetching."

"Reynard, I think you're playing games," she said. "Tell me the truth about how you got away from the King's court."

"Dame, I flattered the King and the Queen so much that I'm thinking our friendship will be on the thin side once he knows about this. He'll be angry and rapidly search me out to hang me by the neck. So let's leave and secretly steal away to some other forest where we can live without fear and dread. There we can live seven years and more, without being found. There is plenty of good food there—partridges and woodcocks and plenty of other wild birds. If you'll come with me, you'll find sweet wells and beautiful, clear-flowing streams—lord knows how sweet the air is there. We can well live peacefully, in ease and plenty. For the King has released me because I told him that there was great treasure in Krekenpit, but he'll find nothing there even if he looked forever. He'll be furious the moment he knows he's been fooled. Imagine how many lies I had to concoct to be free of him. It was an extremely difficult escape. Never have I been harder pressed or closer to death, but no matter how the matter

Then the hare cried, “Help, Benin! Where are you?
This pilgrim is killing me.”

goes now, I'll never come within the King's power again. I've got my thumb out of his mouth, thanks to my subtlety."

"Reynard, I don't think we should leave for another forest," said Dame Ermilyn. "We'd be miserable strangers there. Here we have all we want, and here you're lord of our neighborhood. Why should we leave this place, and risk everything in a worse one? We can stay here securely enough. If the King makes trouble or besieges us, there are so many side holes through which we'll escape from him. In staying here we can't go wrong, since we know all the byways in the district. Before he could capture us with force he'd need a great deal of help. That you have sworn that you'd go overseas is the thing that concerns me most."

"No, wife, don't be worried about that. There's a saying: 'The more forsworn, the more forlorn,'[24] but I once accompanied a good man, who said that a forced oath was no oath. Going on pilgrimage wouldn't help me a cat's tail. I'll stay here and follow your advice. If the King hunts me, I'll manage as best I can. If he's overmighty with me, I still hope to trick him through my subtlety. I'll untie my sack of tricks: if he's looking for trouble, he'll find it."

Now Bellin the Ram was annoyed that Cuwaert his fellow was working so long in the hole, and called out loudly: "Come out, Cuwaert, in the devil's name! How long will Reynard keep you there? Get a move on and let's go!"

When Reynard heard this, he went out and said gently to Bellin the Ram: "Dear Bellin, why so impatient? Cuwaert's talking

24 I have preserved the archaic language here to preserve the rhyme of the proverb, which means, "The more a man betrays a promise, the more wretched he is."

with his dear aunt. It strikes me that you shouldn't be displeased by that. He asked me to suggest to you that you go on ahead, and he'll come on afterwards. He's quicker on foot than you are, and he must stay awhile with his aunt and her children. They're terribly upset that I'm leaving them behind."

"What happened to Cuwaert?" replied Bellin. "I thought I heard him cry out for help."

"What are you talking about, Bellin?" said the fox. "Do you think that any harm could come to him? Now listen to what he did when we entered our house, and when Ermilyn understood that I was to go overseas. She fainted, and when Cuwaert saw that, he cried out loudly: 'Bellin, come help my aunt—bring her out of this faint!' "

The ram then said: "Oh, dear, I'd understood that Cuwaert himself was in great danger."

"No, no, truly," said the fox, "rather than Cuwaert ever come to any harm in my house, I'd prefer my wife and children to suffer a good deal of harm themselves."

21

Reynard sends the head of Cuwaert the Hare to the King, with Bellin as carrier

"Bellin, don't you remember," asked the fox, "that only yesterday the King and his council commanded me to send two letters before I departed this country? Dear cousin, I beg you to take these two letters—they're already written."

The ram replied: "I never knew whether or not your writing and composition were any good. You might have asked me to transport them as long as I had something in which to carry them."

"Fear not: you'll have something to carry them in. Just be sure they're delivered. I'll give you the pouch I carry, and put the letters for the King in that. I'll hang them about your neck, and the King will repay you well. Believe me, he'll be happy to see you."

So Bellin promised to carry the letters. Reynard went back into the house and put Cuwaert's head in the pouch. He entrusted it to Bellin with the aim of endangering him. He hung the pouch about Bellin's neck, and charged him not to look in it, if he wanted to maintain the King's friendship.

"And if you want the King's goodwill and love, tell him that you composed the letter yourself, and suggested how it might be better written and composed. You'll be much admired for it."

Bellin the Ram was happy to hear this, thinking that he'd win much praise.

"Reynard," he said, "I know what a favor you're doing me now. I'll be much praised in court once it's known just how well I can compose a letter. Even though I'm totally incapable of doing that, it's often the case that God permits some people to derive praise and honor from the work of others, which will be my case now. Now, what do you advise, Reynard: Shall Cuwaert the Hare come with me to court?"

"No," said the fox, "he'll follow along soon. He can't yet come, as he's speaking with his aunt. Now you go on ahead, and I'll tell some secrets to Cuwaert."

Bellin bade farewell to Reynard, and went to court, running so fast that he arrived before midday. He found the King and his barons in his palace. The King was astonished when he saw Bellin bringing back the pouch that had been made with the bear's skin.

The King said: "Tell us, Bellin: Where have you come from? Where's the fox? Why doesn't he have the pouch with him?"

"My lord," Bellin replied, "I'll tell you all I know. I accompanied Reynard to his house. When I was ready he asked if I would, for your sake, carry two letters to you. I told him that for your honor and pleasure I would gladly carry seven letters. So he brought this bag to me, in which you'll find the letters. I composed them and gave counsel in their making. I don't believe you'll ever have laid eyes on more skillfully constructed epistles."

So the King commanded Bokart his secretary, who understood all languages, to read the letters. Tybert the Cat and Bokart took the pouch from Bellin's neck.

Bellin had already confessed enough to condemn himself.

The cleric Bokart undid the pouch and pulled out Cuwaert's

head. He said: "What letters are these? My lord, this is most definitely Cuwaert's head!"

"Damn it," said the King, "that I ever believed the fox!"

The grief of both King and Queen was on display for all to see. The King was so angry that he held his head down for a long time. Finally, after much deliberation, he uttered a great cry, so that all the animals were afraid. Then Sir Fineskin the Leopard, who had some kinship with the King, spoke.

"Sir, why make such a noise? You're expressing as much grief as if the Queen were dead. Let this grief pass, and put on a pleasant expression. Act like the lord and King of this land! Doesn't it stand entirely under your command?"

"Sir Fineskin," said the King, "how can I allow this single criminal and treacherous felon to betray me? How can I let him turn against me and anger my friends, stout Bruin the Bear and Isengrim the Wolf? It pains me intensely and runs directly against my honor that I've acted against the interests of my best barons, and that I so completely trusted that false beast the fox. My wife is to blame: she begged me so much that I listened to her. I regret that, even if it's too late."

"What does it matter, Sir King?" said the leopard. "If there's anything amiss, we'll sort it out. We'll give solid recompense to Bruin the Bear, to Isengrim the Wolf, and to Arswind his wife for the patch of skin and for the shoes. As for Bellin the Ram, since he's confessed that he colluded in Cuwaert's death, it's only reasonable that he pay for it now. Let's all go and fetch Reynard. We'll arrest him and hang him there and then, without any due process of law. Everyone will rejoice at that."

22

Bellin the Ram and all his lineage are put into the hands of Isengrim and Bruin. Bellin is killed

The King said that he'd do all this gladly. Fineskin the Leopard then went to the prison and first unbound Bruin and Isengrim. "Sirs," he said, "above all, I bring you pardon and my lord's love and friendship. He's deeply sorry that he's ever spoken or acted in any way against you. You'll have good appointments, as well as recompense. He'll give you Bellin the Ram, along with all his lineage from now to Doomsday. Wherever you find them in a field or forest, they're yours to eat without penalty. The King furthermore grants that you can freely hunt and harass Reynard and all his family to the utmost. The King grants you both this precious privilege to hold from him forever. You are to swear to the King never to wrong him, but to pay him due homage and loyalty. I advise you to accept all this, for you can do it without loss of reputation."

Thus the peace was adroitly reestablished by Fineskin the Leopard. That cost Bellin his fleece along with his life. The wolf's lineage hold these privileges from the King, and to this very day they consume Bellin's descendants wherever they can find them. This dispute was begun in a wicked time, because peace could never be made between the parties after this. The King in his court was so delighted by this peace that he lengthened the feast by twelve days out of love for the bear and the wolf.

23

The King holds his feast. Lapreel the Rabbit accuses Reynard the Fox before the King

To this great feast all manner of animals came, for the King had announced it across the entire land. There was more joy and happiness than was ever seen among the animals. There were courtly dances, with bagpipes, trumpets, and all kinds of minstrelsy. The King ordered so much food that everyone was plentifully served. There was no animal, great or insignificant, who wasn't there, including many birds, and all who desired the King's friendship.

All, that is, except Reynard the Fox, the red, false pilgrim, who lay in wait planning how he could do harm. He judged that his presence would not be appreciated.

There was an abundance of food and drink, and there were plays and diversions. The feast was full of music—anyone would have loved to have seen it.

About midday on the eighth day of the gathering, Lapreel the Rabbit came before the King, where he sat at the table with the Queen. He spoke sorrowfully so that all present could hear him.

"My lord, have pity on my complaint, which concerns the battery and murder that Reynard the Fox wished to inflict on me yesterday morning. I came running through his district Wickedhole. He stood outside his door dressed like a pilgrim. I had thought to have passed him in peace as I came to this feast. When he saw me coming he stepped towards me, saying his prayers.

"I greeted him but he didn't answer a single word. Instead he tripped me with his right foot and struck my head right between my ears. I thought I was about to lose my head, but thanks be to God I was so agile that I sprang from him and agonizingly extracted myself from his claws. He grimaced as if he was angry that he hadn't gripped me more tightly. When I escaped I lost an ear, and my head had four great bleeding gashes from his sharp claws. I nearly fainted, but out of fear for my life I sprang up and ran so quickly away from him that he couldn't catch up. Behold these great wounds, my lord, which he's inflicted on me with his long sharp claws. Pity me and punish this false traitor and murderer, or else no one will be able to pass the heath in safety as long as Reynard cruelly applies his own law.

24

Corbant the Crow accuses the fox of the death of his wife

ust as the rabbit ended his accusation, Corbant the Crow flew into the court right before the King and said: "Dear lord, hear me out. I bring before you a heart-wrenching complaint. This morning I went with my wife Sharpbeak to play on the heath. There lay Reynard the Fox on the ground like a dead wretch. His eyes stared and his tongue hung out of his mouth like a dead dog's. We touched his belly and found no sign of life. Then my wife laid her ear to his mouth to know whether or not he was breathing.

"This turned out very badly for her. For the false, cruel fox bided his time; when he saw her close enough he caught her by the head and bit it off. I was terribly upset by this and loudly cried: 'Oh, dear me, what's going on here!' Then he quickly stood up and snatched so greedily at me that for fear of death I trembled and flew up into a nearby tree. There I saw from afar how the false wretch devoured Sharpbeak so hungrily that he left nothing but a few feathers—no flesh or bone. He even ate the small feathers with the flesh. He was so hungry that he would've even eaten the two eyes, which he normally wouldn't bother with. He then went on his way. I flew down mournfully and gathered the feathers to show them to you here. I'll never again put myself in such danger and fear as I was in then, not for a thousand marks of the finest Arabian gold.

"My lord the King: behold the piteous remains. These are the feathers of Sharpbeak my wife. My lord, if you care about your reputation, then you must enact justice for this. Avenge yourself, so men will fear and respect you. If you permit freedom of movement to be infringed, you yourself won't be able to travel in safety on the highway. God judges lords who fail to do justice and permit the law to be ignored when it comes to thieves, murderers, and lawbreakers as partners in crime. Everyone will be a lord himself. Dear lord: look to it to retain your reputation."

25

The King is terribly angry at these accusations

Noble the King was terribly angry by the time he'd heard the rabbit's and the crow's accusations. He was frightening to see, with his eyes burning like fire. He bellowed as loudly as a bull so that the entire court trembled in fear.

Crying aloud, he finally said, "By my crown and the faithfulness I owe my wife, I'll avenge this crime so that it'll be talked about for a long time! I was a fool so readily to have believed the false scoundrel, and to allow my safe conduct and peace to be broken.

"His false, flattering speech deceived me. He told me that he was going to the Pope in Rome and from there overseas to the Holy Land. I gave him a pouch, a Psalter, and made a pilgrim of him, intending nothing but honest dealing. What tricks he's capable of! How he can stuff his sleeves with contemptible nonsense!

"It was my wife who caused all this trouble—I acted entirely by her counsel. I'm not the first to have been deceived by the advice of women, which has caused many catastrophes.

"I command all who are dependent on me and desire my

"It was my wife who caused all this trouble."

friendship, wherever they may be, to help me with advice and action to avenge this dreadful crime, so that we may continue to live with honor and respectability. This false thief must be shamed so that he never again can infringe our safe conduct. I'll support this effort myself in every way I can!"

Isengrim the Wolf and Bruin the Bear listened carefully to the King's words, and hoped to be avenged on Reynard the Fox. They didn't, however, dare utter a single word. The King was so annoyed that none dared speak.

At last the Queen spoke (in French): "*Sire, pour dieu ne croyez jamais toutes choses que l'on vous dit; et ne jurez pas légèrement*: a man of worship should not instantly believe everything he's told, or swear an oath until he understands the matter clearly. He should rightfully also to listen to the other party's case. There are many who accuse others who are themselves the criminals. *Audi alteram partem*: hear the other party. I truly thought that the fox was honest, and, assuming he meant no treachery, I helped him insofar as I could. However it turns out, whether he's wicked or honest, it strikes me that you should not, for your own honor, proceed against him with undue haste. That would be neither good nor reputable. He can't escape from you. You can imprison or flay him: he must obey your judgment."

Then Fineskin the Leopard said: "My lord, it seems to me that my lady has expressed the truth of the matter and given you good counsel. Do well and follow her, and take the advice of your wise council. If he's found guilty of the alleged crimes that have now come to light, let him be punished heavily for those crimes. And if he doesn't appear before this feast is ended and excuse himself, as he ought to do by right, then do as the council will advise you. Even if he were twice as crooked as he is, I wouldn't counsel that he be punished more than justice stipulates."

"Sir Fineskin, we're all agreed," said Isengrim the Wolf. "As long as the King is pleased, we can't be better off. But for the sake of argument, let's assume that Reynard were present with us now. Let's assume that he'd cleared himself of twice the number of accusations against him here. I'd still argue that he'd forfeited his life. Now, however, I'll keep quiet and not say a thing, because he's absent. Yet in addition to all this he's told the King about a certain treasure lying in Krekenpit in Hulsterloe. Never was there a greater lie. With it he's fooled us all, and has inflicted grievous pain on me and the bear. I'd put my life on it that the whole story is a pack of lies. Right now he's thieving everything that goes past his house on the heath. Nonetheless, Sir Fineskin, whatever pleases the King and you must be right. He could, though, very easily have come, since he knew about it from the King's messenger."

The King said: "We won't send for him in any other way. I order all those who owe me service and who desire my honor and worship to prepare for war at the end of six days. All archers with bows, horsemen and footmen, guns and cannons: all are to be ready to besiege Wickedhole. If I'm any sort of a King, I'll destroy Reynard the Fox. Lords and sires: What do you say to this? Will you do this with a good will?"

"Yes, lord: say the word and we'll go with you!" they all cried.

26

Grimbart the Badger warns Reynard that the King is angry and wants to kill him

rimbart the Badger, Reynard's nephew, heard all this. He was distressed by the turn of events, and ran directly to Wickedhole, not passing around bush or hedge, but rushing so quickly that he was sweating. He was worried for Reynard his red uncle.

As he went he said under his breath: "What danger you're in! What will become of you? Will I see you executed, or else exiled? I've good reason to be anxious, for you're the head of our kin. Your counsel is wise and you're ready to help your friends when they're in trouble. You can also present your case: wherever you speak, you always win."

Weeping and distressed, Grimbart arrived at Wickedhole, where he found his Uncle Reynard. Reynard had caught two pigeons as they made their first flight from the nest to see if they could fly. Because their wings were as yet too short, they fell to the ground, and as Reynard had gone hunting, he'd spotted and captured them. So now he'd brought them home.

When he saw Grimbart coming, Reynard said: "Welcome, nephew, best loved among all my kindred! You've run fast—you're covered in sweat. What's the news?"

"Dear uncle, I'm afraid that you're between a rock and a hard place. You risk losing both life and property. The King has sworn that he'll put you to a shameful death. He's ordered all his people to be ready in six days—archers, footmen, horsemen, and wagoners. He's got guns, cannons, tents, and pavilions. He's also ordered torches to be prepared. Look out, now, for you're in a tight corner. Isengrim and Bruin are closer now to the King than I am to you. They get everything they ask for. Isengrim has made the King believe that you're a thief and a murderer—he hates you. Lapreel the Rabbit and Corbant the Crow have also made accusations. I'm afraid for your life, so much that I'm sick with dread."

"*Pff,*" said the fox, "dear nephew, now, is this all that's troubling you? Are you so afraid of this? Spirits up! Even though the King and all the court had sworn my death, I'll come out on top of the lot of them. They can all chatter and champ and give counsel, but the court can't do anything without me and my wily cleverness."

PART IV

The friends of Reynard the Fox prepare the ground for his escape from all charges

27

Reynard returns to court

"ear nephew, forget about all this and come in. See what I have for you: a good pair of fat pigeons—my favorite food! They're easy to digest and can almost be swallowed whole, since pigeon bones are half blood. I eat flesh and bones all together, since I don't digest easily without light food. My wife Ermilyn will welcome us graciously, but don't discuss the business at court: she's so tenderhearted she'd take it badly. The fear might make her ill. A small thing goes directly to her heart. And tomorrow, first thing, I'll go with you to court. As long as I can speak and be heard, I'll answer them so that I'll touch some near enough. Friend, will you stand by me as a friend ought to?"

"Yes, truly, dear uncle," said Grimbart, "my life and everything I own is all yours."

"God reward you, nephew. That's well said. If I live I'll repay you."

"Uncle," said Grimbart, "you might well be able to appear before all the lords and get off. As long as you can speak, no one will be able to arrest or detain you. The Queen and the leopard have settled that."

"Then," said the fox, "I'm glad of it. I don't give a penny for the best of them. I'll save my neck."

They spoke no more about this matter, but went into the fortress, and found Ermilyn, who, sitting there by her young, stood up immediately and welcomed them courteously. Grimbart greeted his aunt and the children warmly, and the two pigeons that Reynard had caught were readied for supper. Each took their helping, and there wasn't a thing left over.

The fox said: "Dear nephew, how do you like my children Rosel and Reynkin?—they'll be sure to bring honor to our lineage. They're growing up beautifully: one catches a chicken and the other a pullet. They can also duck in the water after plovers and ducks. I'd send them often for game, but first I want to teach them how to protect themselves from hunters' traps and dogs. If they get smart, I'm confident that they'll provide us with lots of good and diverse food that we don't have right now. They like and follow me well, for they can play angry, and when they hate someone they can appear friendly and lighthearted. With these tricks they bring prey underfoot and bite throats clean in two. This is the fox's nature. They're certainly eloquent speakers, which pleases me well."

"Uncle," said Grimbart, "congratulations on having such smart kids. I'm happy about them myself, because they're my kin."

"Grimbart, you've been sweating and are exhausted, it's high time you took a rest."

That struck Grimbart as a first-rate idea, so they lay down on a litter of straw. The fox, his wife, and his children all went to sleep. Reynard was, however, unsettled. He sighed and thought obsessively about how he could get out of all this.

The following morning he and Grimbart left the castle. First, though, he said goodbye to Ermilyn his wife and to his children: "I won't be away long. I have to go with Cousin Grimbart to court. Don't worry if I don't come back straightaway. If you hear any bad news, don't be troubled by it. Watch out for yourselves and protect our castle. I'll do as best I can in court once I see how things look there."

"Say it isn't so, Reyner," said Ermilyn. "Why have you now decided to return to court? The last time you went there you were in lethal danger. And you said you'd never go there again."

"Wife," said the fox, "the chances of this world are mysterious: thinking often turns out to be wrong, and many a person thinks he'll have a thing that he ends up not getting. I have to go. Don't give it a thought—the whole business is safe as houses. I hope to come back within five days at the most."

With that Reynard and Grimbart left for court. When it got hot, Reynard said: "Nephew, since I was last forgiven of my sins, I've been a very bad boy. I'd like you now to hear me confess all my sins.

"I caused the bear to end up with a terrible wound for the pouch that was cut out of his skin. I made the wolf and his wife lose their shoes. I pacified the King with a bundle of lies and fooled him into believing that the wolf and the bear would have betrayed him and killed him. I provoked the King's anger against them when they didn't deserve it. I also told the King that there was an enormous treasure in Hulsterloe, for which he'll never be better off or richer, because all that was nothing but baloney. I led Bellin the Ram and Cuwaert the Hare with me, killed Cuwaert, and then mockingly sent Cuwaert's head to the King with Bellin. And I bit the rabbit between the ears and almost killed him, but he was so quick he escaped. The crow may well accuse me, because I swallowed Dame Sharpbeak his wife.

"I also forgot one thing last time I confessed to you, which has troubled me since. What I'm about to tell you was truly deceitful. I came walking with the wolf, between Houthulst and Elverdinge. There we saw a red mare with a good, fat black colt of about four-months. Isengrim was ravenous, and asked me to go to the mare to ask whether or not she'd sell her colt. I ran to the horse and posed the question, to which she said that she'd sell the colt for money. Asked how much, she told me that the sum was written on her back hoof. 'If you're a scholar, you can come and read it.'

"I then understood her tactic entirely, and said: 'Not me, because unfortunately I can't read. Besides, it's not me who wants to buy your child. Isengrim has sent me here and wants to know the price.'

"The mare said: 'Let him come himself, then. I'll let him have all the facts he wants.'

" 'I'm on it,' I said, and went directly to Isengrim and said: 'Dear uncle, do you want to fill your belly with that colt? If so, go to the mare who's waiting for you. She has the price of her colt written under her foot. She wanted me to read it, but I'm afraid I can't read. I'm very sorry about being illiterate. I never went to school. Uncle, if you want the colt, and if you can read, then that colt is yours.'

" 'Of course, nephew, I can read very well. That won't stop me for a second—I know French, Latin, English, and German. I went to school in Oxford.[25] I've also been in the audience when old and wise doctors of law pronounced on pleas and gave sen-

25 From the twelfth century onward Oxford was one of the great Northern European centers of university learning.

tence. I'm licensed myself in both civil and canon law, and I can read texts as readily as I can read my name in whatever text any man might compose. I'll go and get the price.'

"So he asked me to wait for him, and he ran off to the mare and asked her whether or not she'd sell her foal.

"She replied: 'The sum is written on my foot.'

" 'Then let me read it.'

" 'Do,' she said, at which point she lifted her hoof, newly shod with iron and strong nails. With it she kicked him square in the head, and he fell like a dead man. Anyone would have been able to ride a mile or two before he got up.

"The mare trotted away with her colt, leaving Isengrim lying wounded in terrible pain. He lay and bled and howled like a dog. I went to him and said: 'Sir Isengrim, dear uncle, how're things with you? Have you eaten your fill of the colt? Is your belly full? How come you don't give me any? After all, I ran your errand. Have you slept your dinner off? Come on and tell me what was written under the mare's hoof. What was it—prose or rhyme, meter and verse? I'd love to know. I believe it was melodic, for I thought I heard you sing from a ways off. You know so much that no one could read it as well as you.'

" 'Please, please, Reynard!' said the wolf. 'Cut the mockery right now. I'm in such a bad way and so painfully wounded that someone with a heart of stone would pity me. The whore with her long leg had an iron foot. I thought the nails were letters and she inflicted five wounds with the first strike to my head, which is almost broken. I never want to read letters like those ones again.'

" 'Dear uncle, are you telling me the truth? I'm amazed, since I thought you were one of the most learned scholars alive. Now I know for sure that what I've often read and heard is true: "The best scholars are not the wisest men." The unlearned sometimes become wise themselves. Scholars aren't the wisest, because they study so much in learned stuff and science that they grow stupid.'

"Thus I led Isengrim into this great, dangerous trap, so that he hardly came away alive.

"Dear nephew, now I've recounted to you all the sins I can remember. Whatever might happen in court—I have no idea how it will turn out there—I'm not so afraid now. For I'm clear from sin, and I'm happy to receive whatever merciful penance you judge fit."

Grimbart declared that the sins were serious, but the dead must nonetheless remain dead. "I therefore forgive you everything, even if I'm worried that you'll suffer before you can wriggle out of the murder charge. I absolve you here and now.

"The biggest obstacle you'll face will be having sent Cuwaert's head to court, and having blinded the King with such lies—uncle, that wasn't such a smart idea."

The fox replied: "Dear nephew, when we pass through this world, we hear this, and we see that. We reflect on what we see and hear, but we can't respond to all our experience straightforwardly. How on earth should anyone handle honey without licking his fingers? My conscience often roars at me and pricks me to love God above all things, and to love my fellow Christians as myself, as is entirely acceptable to God, and in keeping with his law.

"But just think how reason fights against what we want. When I'm overcome by desire for what I want it seems that I've lost my head, and don't know what's troubling me. I get in such a muddle. But now I've been forgiven all my sins and hate all that's sinful. I'm rising to high contemplation above God's commandments, and I'll achieve this special grace only when I'm alone.

A short while afterwards, when I return to the world, I find so many obstacles, and I find the tracks in which those corrupt prelates and rich priests move in, I'm caught again. The world returns to me and will have me for itself. The flesh wants to live in pleasure, and puts so many temptations in my way that my good thoughts and intentions vanish completely. Instead of good thoughts I hear singing, piping, laughing, playing, and a great deal of jollity. I hear that the prelates and rich curates preach one thing, but think and do altogether another. So I learn the lies that are most commonly found in the courts of nobles.

"Lords, ladies, priests, and scholars are the biggest liars. Men daren't tell lords the truth now. Where there's a failing, I must flatter and lie, or else have the door shut on me. I've often heard men say the truth, who with a lie make their argument conform better to their intention. They have to mix the lie in to add a flourish to their case. Often the lie comes spontaneously, and falls in with the matter without premeditation. So when the lie is well dressed, it falls into step with the truth.

"Dear nephew, men must now lie here, and tell the truth there. They have to flatter, threaten, beg, and curse. They must attack their opponent's weakest point. Whoever intends to prosper in the world without composing a beautiful lie, without wrapping it and hiding it so that men take it for truth, won't escape servitude. If a man is so subtle as not to stammer when he's being heard, nephew, he can work wonders. He'll wear scarlet and fur, he'll win in both canon and civil law and wherever he has business to do.

"There are many treacherous people now who want to hold on to their advantages. They think they know how to lie well and they presume to lie. Such people prefer to eat of the juiciest morsels, but they aren't trusted or heard out. And there are many who are so fat and foolish that they lose their grip on the task in hand, when it comes to making a concluding argument. They can't help themselves, and leave their legal case without top or bottom. Such a person is considered a fool and there are many who laugh at him. But the man who can supply a fit conclusion to his lie, and express it without faltering, as if it were all written out in front of him, and can blind his listeners so that his lie is taken for truth—now, that's your man.

"What special skill does it take to tell the truth? How these false and deceptive tricksters laugh who construct lies and deceptively manage to suppress truth. They're able to compose petitions and insert matter that was never thought or spoken. They teach men to see through their fingers. They do all this only to win money. They put their tongues out to hire to maintain and strengthen their lies. I'm afraid, nephew, that this is a most wicked skill, which can produce death and damage.

"I don't deny that men must trick, play, and lie in small matters, for whoever always says the truth never prospers in the world at all. There are many who say whatever their masters want to hear. Whoever always tells the truth will find many obstacles. Men can lie when they need to and afterwards correct the matter by skill. Mercy is available for all sins. No man is so wise that he never makes a mistake."

"Well, dear uncle, what'll block you?" said Grimbart. "You know all situations down to the finest grain. You quickly leave me behind. Your arguments surpass my understanding. Why do you need absolution? By rights you should be the priest yourself! You should allow me and other members of the flock to come to *you* for forgiveness. You understand the ways of the world so well that no one can deceive you."

Talking in this way, they walked into court. The fox was a bit anxious, but put on a brave face all the same. He marched directly through the crowd to the place where the King himself was. Grimbart remained by the fox's side and said: "Don't be afraid, uncle. Put on a bold front. Fortune favors the brave. Often a single day is more productive than a whole year."

"You're right there, nephew," said the fox. "May God repay you for the comfort you give me."

And so on he went, looking aggressively here and there, as if to say: *What do you want? Here I come!* He saw many of his kin there who wished him little good, such as the otter, the beaver, and up to ten others, whom I shall name in good time. Some were there who loved him.

The fox entered, fell down on his knees before the King, and spoke.

28

Reynard excuses himself in the King's presence

"Nothing is hidden from God, who stands above all in power. I ask God to preserve my lord the King and my lady the Queen, and to give the King grace to know who has right on his side and who is in the wrong. The outward appearance of many people differs entirely from what they're secretly thinking. I wish God would openly show each man's misdeeds and that each man's crimes stood written on his forehead, even if it cost me more than I can now say. And I wish that you, my lord, knew as much as I do—and how I set myself both early and late to your service. In return for that service, accusations are directed at me by the malevolent. By lies I'm exiled from your grace and good valuation. My enemies charge me unjustly with great crimes, contrary to justice.

"Against those who've so falsely maligned me and brought me into such a predicament, I declare my innocence, even though I know both you, my lord, and you, my lady, are people of great wisdom and discrimination who won't be led to believe lies such as these. It's not your custom to do so. Therefore, dear lord, I implore you wisely to consider every detail of this case with legal judgment. By word and deed, I ask only that every man be treated according to justice. Let the guilty be convicted and punished. Men will know well now, before I leave this court, who I am. I'm unable to flatter, and will always openly show the truth of the matter."

Everyone in the court was still, and all were amazed that the fox spoke with such courage. "Ha—Reynard," said the King, "how well you pitch your lies and make your opening gambits, but your eloquence won't help you this time. I'm certain that you'll be hanged for your crimes today. I won't tell you off. Instead I'll shorten your pain. You've shown how much you love us through your treatment of Lapreel the Rabbit and Corbant the Crow. Your lies and treacherous inventions will bring you directly to death. A pot may go to water only until it finally comes home broken. I think your pot, which has so often deceived us, is about to be broken now."

Reynard was afraid of what the lion was saying. He'd much rather have been at Cologne than at the King's court.[26] But he knew that he had to carry on.

"My lord the King, whatever I do," he said, "you'd be well advised to let me speak. Even if I were condemned to death, you ought to hear me out. Before now I've given you excellent, effective counsel. I've always stayed at your side when you needed me, while the other animals failed and abandoned you. If the wicked with their fake stories have now wrongfully slandered me to you so that I'm unable to excuse myself, then don't I have the right to complain?

26 Here meaning, "He'd have much rather been somewhere else than at the king's court." Cologne is in central-western Germany, near Aachen, which is mentioned earlier.

"In earlier episodes I've seen that I should be heard openly. The current state of affairs might nonetheless change, and return to the way it was. Good deeds of yore should be remembered. I see in front of me many of my kin and friends who seem to want nothing to do with me just now, even though it would pain them inwardly if you, my lord King, should execute me wrongfully. In doing so you'd be destroying the most faithful servant you have in these lands.

"What do you think, Sir King? Had I known myself guilty or at fault in any action, would I have come here to face the law in the presence of all my enemies? No, sir, not for all the red gold in the world! I was free and at my liberty. Why should I have come here? God knows, I am wholly innocent of any transgression, so much so that I dare come here in broad daylight, and I dare answer to any charge that's laid on me. When Grimbart first brought news of these proceedings to me, I was beside myself with distress. I fell about here and there like a madman. If I hadn't been under the curse of the Church, I would've come right away. So I went on grieving on the heath, and was so distressed I didn't know what to do. Then it so happened that I met Mertin the Ape, my uncle, who'd been attorney for the Bishop of Camerik for nine years. He's much smarter in learned matters than most priests.

"He could see I was hurting badly, and said: 'Dear cousin, it seems to me that you aren't yourself. What's up? Who's giving you grief? Something that's troubling you deeply should be shared with friends. A friend in need is a friend in deed. A friend often finds a better solution than the defendant. For the person charged with serious accusations is so depressed by them that he's often unable to think his way out of them. Such people are so despondent that they seem to have lost their wit.'

"I said: 'Dear uncle, you're right. I've succumbed to the very condition you describe. Without deserving anything, I'm thrown into a deep hole, and by someone to whom I've always been a stout and faithful friend. I'm speaking about the rabbit who came to me yesterday morning as I sat outside my house saying morning prayers. He told me he was off to court and greeted me in a friendly way, and so I returned the greeting. He then said this to me: "Good Reynard, I'm hungry and weary. You wouldn't by any chance have some food, would you?" "Sure," I said, "plenty, come in!"

" 'So I gave him a couple of slices of the finest wheat bread with sweet butter. It was a Wednesday, when I'm unaccustomed to eat any flesh. And so I fasted because the feast of Pentecost wasn't far off. For those who will taste of the highest wisdom and live the most spiritual lives, as they keep the Lord's Ten Commandments, must fast and prepare for the high feasts of the Church: *Et vos estote parati.*[27] Dear uncle, I gave him beautiful white bread with sweet butter, with which a hungry man might well find relief.

" 'When he'd eaten his fill, then Reynkin my youngest son turned up and wanted to take the leftovers. Young children are always hungry. But once he reached out to take something, the rabbit hit Russell on his mouth so that his teeth bled and he dropped down in a faint. When Reynardin my eldest son saw that, he sprang to the rabbit and caught him by the head. He would have killed him if I hadn't rescued him. Lapreel repaid my charity by roughly thrashing my child. And then he ran to the King and announced that I wanted to murder him! Do you not

27 "And you, be ready . . ." (Matthew 24:44).

see, uncle, how I'm slandered and laid in blame? And yet he's the one complaining, not me!

" 'After the business with Lapreel, Corbant the Crow flew up, making a self-pitying racket. I asked him what the problem was. "My wife is dead! There's a dead hare over there, full of maggots and worms. She ate so much of it that the worms have bitten her throat in two." I asked him how that could possibly happen, but he wouldn't say another word and flew off and left me there. And now he's saying that *I* bit and killed her! How could I get near enough to her? She can fly, whereas I go on foot. So now you have it, dear Uncle Mertin: you see how I'm treated. I sure am unlucky. But perhaps it's because of my old sins. It would do me good if I could endure it patiently.'

"The ape said to me: 'Nephew, you must go to court and appear in front of the lords to get out of this.'

" 'I'm afraid, uncle, that simply can't happen. The archdeacon has put the curse of the Church on me, because I counseled Isengrim the Wolf to abandon his monastic life at Elmare. Isengrim complained to me that he lived so austerely, what with all the long fasting, the reading, and all that singing, that he simply couldn't stomach it a moment longer. He'd die if he was forced to stick with it. I pitied him, and helped him as a true friend, and so he abandoned his calling. I'm deeply sorry I did this, now that he's working away as hard as he can to have me hanged by the King. He repays my good deed with nasty payment. So you see, uncle, I'm at my wits' end and have no idea what to do. I'm obliged to go to Rome for absolution. But if I do, then my wife and children will be harmed and dishonored. These malicious beasts who hate me will inflict all the damage they can to my family, and drive them wherever they're able. I'd defend my family if I were free of the papal curse, for then I'd go to court and give an account of myself. But now I daren't—I'd be in a state of sin if I came before good people, and I'd be afraid that God would punish me.'

" 'No, cousin,' said my uncle the ape, 'don't be afraid. I won't leave you in this bind. I know the way to Rome very well. I understand how this works, for I'm well known there and I'm known there as the clerk of Bishop Mertyn. I'll accuse the archdeacon and enter a plea against him, and I'll return with an absolution for you, despite the archdeacon.[28] I know how to manage this, since Simon my uncle lives in Rome, and he's a powerful guy.[29] He immediately helps whoever can give anything. There you'll find Take-it-all, Harm-watch, and other friends and allies of mine. I'll also take some money with me if I need any, for a petition grows stronger when it's backed up by gifts. Justice is always moved forward with a little cash. A faithful friend risks both life and property for his friend, and that's what I'll do for you in your just cause.

" 'So cheer up, cousin! I won't rest after tomorrow until I'm in Rome, where I'll look out for your business. And you go to court as soon as you can. I'll absolve you of all your sins that brought you under the Pope's curse. I'll take care of them. When you come to court you'll find Rukenawe my wife, her two sisters, my three children, and many more of our kin. Dear cousin: you can speak to them in confidence. My wife is as wise as they come.

28 The male ape is a thoroughly corrupt figure, who promises to interfere with the processes of justice by bribing ecclesiastical figures. An archdeacon is an assistant to a bishop, one of whose responsibilities is the management of church courts.

29 A satirical reference to the practice of simony, the selling of church offices, so named after Simon Magus, who offered payment in return for spiritual power (Acts 8:9-18).

She'll happily help friends. Whoever needs help will find a friend in her. One must always look to his friends, even if he's angered them in the past. Blood must creep on its stomach where it can't walk tall.

" 'If it happens that you are overwhelmed and unable to get justice, then send for me and let me know what's going on. I'll bring everyone in the land—the whole lot of them, be it King or Queen, wife or man—under the Pope's curse. No priest will read, sing, christen children, bury the dead, or administer any sacrament until you get the justice you deserve. I'll manage this, cousin. The Pope is so extremely old that no one much bothers with him. It's Cardinal Puregold who runs things in the papal court—he's young, with lots of friends and a concubine whom he's mad about. What she wants she gets, and quick-smart, believe me. You see, cousin, she's my niece, and I have a good deal of sway there, so that I can get what I want myself, and with bonuses. So bid my lord the King that he does the just thing by you. I know he won't deny you, for justice is a serious undertaking for every man.'

"My lord the King, I sure laughed when I heard this, and with a sense of relief came here, where I've told you the whole truth. If there's anyone in this court who can indict me on a single matter, with good witness, and prove it, as ought to be done in the case of a nobleman, then let me make amends according to the law. If my accuser will not be satisfied with that, then set the day and place and I'll make my innocence good on him, as long as he's of as high a birth as I am and comparable in social status. Whoever can win honor on the battlefield, then let him have it. This is the law that's stood to date, and I don't want it ignored on my account. Law and justice do no man wrong."

All the animals, both poor and rich, were still when the fox spoke so confidently. The rabbit Lapreel and the crow were so terrified that they didn't dare speak a word. They both withdrew from court.

Once they were on the plain, clear of the court, they said: "God give this murderer his comeuppance! He can disguise and hide his falsehood, so that his words seem like gospel truth. No one knows this better than we do. How on earth should we get hold of witnesses? It's better for us to leave court than get caught up in open battle with him. He's so cunning—even if there were five of us we couldn't defend ourselves. He'd kill us all."

Isengrim the Wolf and Bruin the Bear were distressed when they saw these two quit court.

The King said: "If any man wants to accuse Reynard, let him come up and we'll hear him out. Yesterday so many came—where are they now? Reynard is here."

The fox said: "My lord, many accuse who, when they see their adversary, stay mum and drop the charge. Look at Lapreel the Rabbit and Corbant the Crow, who accused me before you in my absence. Now that I'm here, they disappear, and don't dare stand by their own words. If men believe deceptive scoundrels, it's good men who suffer the consequences. To my mind, it's not a good idea to believe characters such as these. Nevertheless, my lord, if by your commandment they'd asked forgiveness from me, then regardless of the magnitude of their crimes, I would've pardoned and forgiven them for your sake. I won't be uncharitable, and neither will I hate or complain about my enemies. Instead I put all things in God's hands. He'll take vengeance on my false accusers as it suits him."

The King said: "Reynard, you look as if you're sincerely in

deep distress, as you say. But are you really as you seem to the world? The matter isn't at all as clear and straightforward as you make out. I am obliged to express my own personal grief. In this case, your own honor and life is at stake.

"You committed a disgraceful and shameful crime when I'd pardoned you all your offenses and you promised to go abroad on pilgrimage. I gave you a pouch and a staff. You later sent the pouch back to me, by Bellin the Ram, with Cuwaert's head in it. What more reprehensible crime could you commit? How on earth were you so foolhardy as to dare shame me thus? Isn't it disgraceful to send a servant's head to a lord? You can't say a word against this, for Bellin the Ram, our former chaplain, told us the whole story. Unless justice fails, you'll have the same reward that he had when he carried the message to us."

Reynard was so afraid, he didn't know what to say. He was at his wits' end, and looked desperately around him, only to see many of his kin and allies who heard everything but said nothing. He was white as a sheet, but no one offered him hand or foot to help.

The King said: "You subtle and false scoundrel, why don't you respond? Has the cat got your tongue?"

The fox stood in great fear and sighed so deeply that everyone heard him. The wolf and the bear rejoiced.

29

Rukenawe the She-Ape answers on behalf of the fox to the King

Dame Rukenawe the She-Ape, Reynard's aunt, wasn't at all happy about the way things were going. She was an intimate of the Queen, and well loved by her. It was lucky for the fox that she was there, for she was very canny, and she had the courage to speak well when it was appropriate. Everyone was relieved when she was present.

"My lord the King," she said, "you really shouldn't sit in judgment when you're angry. It doesn't befit Your Majesty. A man who sits in judgment should put all anger aside. Whoever sits in judgment must preserve his power of discrimination. I know points of law better than some who wear furred gowns.[30] For I learned many such points, and became an expert in law.

"In the Pope's palace at Woerden I had a good bed of hay, while the other animals lay on hard ground. Whenever I wished to speak there, I was allowed to do so, and was heard before others, because I knew the law so well. Seneca writes that a lord must everywhere enact justice.[31] He shall not indict anyone under his

30 The professional garb of lawyers.

31 Lucius Annaeus Seneca (4 BCE–65 CE), the Roman Stoic moral philosopher.

jurisdiction beyond the limit of the law. Law must not favor persons.[32]

"If everyone present here would closely consider what he's done in his time, he'd more readily pity Reynard. Let every man know himself: that's my counsel. No one stands so securely that he can't fall or trip. The man who never committed a crime or a sin is holy and good and has no need to amend himself. But when a man does sin, and amends it by humane counsel, that's as it should be. Always to sin and not to amend oneself is evil—it's diabolical, in fact. Note what is written in the gospel: '*Estote misericordes*': Be merciful; and yet there's more: '*Nolite iudicare et non iudicabimini*': Judge no man and you shall not be judged.[33] I could also cite the passage where the Pharisees brought in the woman taken in adultery, whom they wished to stone to death. They asked our Lord what he thought about this. He said: 'Whichever of you is without sin, let him cast the first stone.' Not a single man remained, but left her standing there.

"We have the same situation here: there are many who see a mote in the eye of another, who don't see the beam in their own eye.[34] There are many who judge others when they are the worst themselves. If one often stumbles, but finally rises up and seeks mercy, he's not damned. God welcomes all those who seek His mercy. Let no man condemn another, even if they know that the person accused has gone amiss. Let them instead look to their own faults, and first correct themselves. If we follow this rule, then my cousin Reynard shouldn't suffer, for his father and

32 Colossians 3:35.

33 Matthew 7:1.

34 A reference to Matthew 7:3.

grandfather have always been held in higher estimation in this court than Isengrim the Wolf or Bruin the Bear, along with all their friends and kin.

"There's always been a striking difference between the wisdom of Reynard my cousin and the honor he's brought this court, on the one hand, and the counsel of Isengrim and Bruin, on the other. They don't have a clue how the world works. So it seems to me that this court is turned upside down: these deceptive, flattering scoundrels rise with promotion and grow powerful among the lords, while the good, the loyal, and the wise are demoted. The loyal have habitually offered true counsel to advance the King's honor. I can't see how we can carry on for long in this way."

"Madam, if he'd wronged you as he's wronged others, you'd grieve for it," the King replied. "Is it any wonder that I hate him? He's always breaking my legal protections. Haven't you heard the accusations against him that have been made here—accusations of murder, theft, and treason? Do you trust him so much? You seem to think he's so innocent, and set him up on an altar to be prayed to like a saint. But no one in the world can say a good word for him. You can say as much as you like for him, but in the end you'll find him worthless, for he's so sunk in crime that he's got no kin or protector or friend who'll venture to help him. I'm surprised at you, because apart from you I never heard of anyone who had an alliance with him who thanked him or put in a good word for him. He always ends up striking them with his tail."

The she-ape answered: "My lord, I love him and consider him a loving friend. I also know of a good deed that he once did in your presence, for which you could repay him with thanks. Even though things have now taken another turn, in the end the heaviest shall weigh most. One must love one's friend with measure, and likewise not hate one's enemy immoderately. Lords should show appropriate steadiness and constancy. One should not praise the day too much until night comes. Good counsel is well spent on him who follows it."

30

A parable of a man who saved a serpent from death

"Two years ago a man and a serpent came to this court to seek judgment. The case was tricky for you and your court. The serpent was stuck in a hedge through which he'd intended to go, but was caught in a trap by the neck, so that without help he couldn't escape, but was likely to lose his life. The man passed by, to whom the serpent called and prayed, asking him to help him out of the snare, or else he'd die.

"The man took pity on him and said: 'If you promise me that you'll not poison me nor do me any harm whatsoever, I'll release you from this trap.' The serpent was ready and swore an oath that he wouldn't harm or hurt the man now or later.

"So the man unloosed the serpent from the snare and they went forth together for a fair time, until the serpent was hungry, since he'd not eaten for a long time. The serpent struck at the man as if he would have killed him. The frightened man started backwards and said: 'What! Will you now kill me? Have you forgotten the oath that you made to me that you wouldn't harm me in any way?'

"The serpent answered: 'What I do is just in the view of the whole world. The necessity provoked by hunger causes a man to break his oath.'

"To which the man replied: 'If that's how you see it, give me as long a delay as it takes to find someone who can judge the matter justly.'

"The serpent granted this request, and off they went together again, until they found Tiselin the Raven and Slyndpere his son. They rehearsed their arguments. Tiselyn the Raven judged immediately that the snake should eat the man. He and his son would've gladly eaten their part of the man too.

"So the serpent said to the man: 'How about it? What do you think? It looks like I've won.'

"The man replied: 'How can a thief judge this case? He'd need to consult others. This is a lone judgment. There should be at least two or three judges together, and they must each understand and enact justice and law. I don't recognize the sentence delivered.'

"They agreed and went on together until they found the bear and the wolf, to whom they recounted their case. These two also judged that the serpent should kill the man, for the need provoked by hunger always trumps any oath.

"The man was then really afraid, as the serpent approached him spitting venom. He just managed to leap aside, and said: 'You're doing me a great injustice, lying in wait to kill me. You've no right to do this!'

"The serpent said: 'Isn't it enough? Our case has been judged twice.'

" 'Yes,' said the man, 'but by those who rob and murder. Everything they swear to they ignore. So I appeal this matter to a court before our lord the King, whose judgment you can't ignore. I'll accept and suffer whatever judgment is given in his court, and never do anything contrary to it.'

"The bear and the wolf agreed to this plan, and the serpent desired nothing better. They imagined that if the case should come before you, lord King, it would proceed exactly as they wished. I believe you remember this yourself very well.

"So they all came to court before you. The wolf's two children came with their father. These were called Empty Belly and Never Full, because they wished to eat the man. They howled for hunger, for which reason you commanded them to void the court. The man, standing in great fear, appealed to your good grace. He recounted how the serpent, whose life he'd saved, wished, against his oath, to kill and devour him.

"The serpent replied: 'I've not committed any crime, and I put my case wholly before the King. I did it to save my life, and to save one's life one can break one's oath and promise.'

"My lord, you and all your council were stymied in this case. For Your Grace could see the man suffering, and you didn't wish to see him sentenced to death for his generosity and kindness. On the other hand, hunger and the need to save one's life must be respected. There was no one in the court who could devise a just decision in this case. There were some who wished that the man was helped—I can see them standing here now. I know very well that they said they couldn't bring this matter to a conclusion.

"You then ordered Reynard my nephew to offer his counsel in the matter. At that time he was trusted above all others in court. You ordered him to deliver a just judgment, and that we should all obey him, because he knew the grounds of law.

"This is what Reynard said: 'My lord, a just decision according to the words used is impossible, for there are often many lies embedded in what men say. If, however, I could see the serpent in the same danger that he was in when the man saved him, then

I'd know exactly what I'd say. Whoever did otherwise would be acting against justice.'

"Then you, my lord, said this: 'Well spoken, Reynard! We agree to it, for no man can say better.'

"So the man and the serpent went to the place where the man first found the serpent. Reynard ordered the serpent to be set back in the snare, just as he had been. And it was done. Then you, my lord, said: 'Reynard, what now? What judgment shall we give?'

"Reynard replied: 'My lord, now they're both in the same position as they were before. They've neither won nor lost. Now take note, my lord, of how I make a just decision exactly to please Your Noble Grace. If the man will now release the serpent from the snare, convinced by the oath that the serpent made to him previously, then he is perfectly free to do that. If, however, the man thinks that he'd be in any way put at a disadvantage by the snake, or if he thinks that the snake would break his oath under provocation of hunger, then I judge that the man may go freely wherever he wants to. In that case he should leave the serpent trapped, just as he could have done when he first came across him. The man could help the serpent out of such extreme danger, and the serpent could break his oath and promise. This therefore strikes me as the just decision: that the man should exercise his free choice, as he did earlier.'

"My lord, this judgment then impressed you and all your attendant council as a good one. You followed it, and praised the wisdom of Reynard, who liberated the man justly. The fox sagely preserved your noble honor, as a faithful servant is bound to do for his lord. When has the bear or the wolf ever performed such noble service? They know well enough how to disguise and shield themselves, to steal and to rob, and to eat fat morsels and fill their bellies. They think it just and lawful that petty thieves who steal hens and chickens should be hanged, whereas they, who steal cows, oxen, and horses, go free as lords. They appear wise as Solomon, Avicenna, or Aristotle,[35] and they demand to be considered worthy and courageous, and to be praised for their prowess. But let them once be where action is required, and they're the first to take off. At that point the powerless have to go in the vanguard, whereas these characters run to the rear.

"My good lord, these and others like them aren't wise. Instead they destroy towns, castles, lands, and whole peoples. They don't give a penny for whose house is on fire, as long as they can warm themselves by the coals. They do nothing but pursue their own interest and selfish advantage. Reynard, by contrast, along with his friends and kin, grieves. Reynard and his kin put honor, advantage, profit, and wise counsel, which is often more valuable than the pride and boasting of their lord, above their own interests. Reynard does all this, despite getting no thanks for it. At the end of the day it'll be known who is best and who works best for the Kingdom.

"My lord, you say that his kin have all withdrawn their support from him, because of his subtle and deceptive tricks. I wish someone else had said that, for then we could take vengeance on the speaker. The traitor would regret the day he ever laid eyes on Reynard. But lord, we shall forbear you—you can say whatever you please. I won't say anything critical about you: if there were

35 Three philosophical figures from three different traditions, respectively King Solomon of Israel (tenth century BCE); Avicenna (Ibn Sina; ca. 980–1037 CE), the Persian philosopher; and the Greek Aristotle (384–322 BCE).

any here who'd prosecute you by any word or deed, we'd resist him sure enough. Where a fight's to be had, we tend not to be afraid.

"But by your leave, my lord, I can easily let you know about Reynard's friends and kin. There are many of them who will risk their life and property for his sake. I declare myself one of them. I am a wife. If he needed me to do so, I'd readily offer up my life and property for him. I also have three adult children, each courageous and strong, whom I'd risk for love of Reynard, so well do I love him, rather than see him destroyed, even though I'd rather die than see them come to harm."

31

The friends and kin of Reynard the Fox

"The first child is Byteluys, who is much loved and playfully active. That's why we give him hefty helpings and lots of good food, which also profits Fulrompe his brother. My third child is a daughter called Hatenette. She's good at picking lice and nits from men's hair. These three are loyal to each other, and I love them dearly."

Dame Rukenawe summoned them and said: "Welcome, my dear children—come up and stand by your beloved nephew."

She then said: "Come along, all you who're kin to me and to Reynard. Let's beg the King to do the right thing by Reynard according to the law of the land."

Many beasts then came up, such as the squirrel, the weasel, the polecat, the martin, the beaver with his wife Ordegale, the mongoose, the stoat, and the ferret —these last two ate poultry as readily as did Reynard. The otter came up with Pantecroet his wife, whom I almost forgot, even if they'd been, along with the beaver, enemies of the fox before. They didn't dare resist Dame Rukenawe, for they were frightened of her. She was the wisest of his kin in giving counsel, and the most feared. More than twenty others stepped forward, out of fear of Rukenawe, to stand by Reynard. Dame Atrote came forward with her two sisters, the weasel and Hermel the Ass. The bat, the water rat, and many others to the number of forty all came up to stand by Reynard the Fox.

"My lord the King," said Rukenawe, "observe whether or not Reynard has any friends. Here you can see that we are your faithful subjects who'd risk life and goods for you in need. Although you're courageous and powerful, our benevolent friendship couldn't harm you. Allow Reynard the Fox to meditate on the matters you've laid against him. If he's unable to prove his innocence himself, then we desire no better than that you do him justice. By right no man should be deprived of the right of self-defense."

The Queen then spoke. "I said all this to the King yesterday, but he was so fierce and angry that he refused to listen."

The leopard also spoke: "Sir, you may judge no further than your men's verdict allows. For if you proceed by willfulness and brute force alone, you'd disgrace yourself. To preserve your dignity, always be certain to hear both sides. Then, by the wisest and best advice give judgment, using your good judgment according to the highest standards of justice."

The King said: "This is all true, but I was so furious when I was told of Cuwaert's death, and saw his head, that I was passionate and rash. I'll hear the fox. If he can answer and prove that he is innocent of the charges against him, I'll gladly let him go scot-free. Further, I'm also moved by the request of his good friends and kin."

Reynard was feeling good at this turn of events, and thought to himself: *God repay my aunt: she's made the branch blossom again. She's helped me out of a very tight spot, and I now have a good foot to dance on. I'll now look directly at my enemies, and produce the most beautiful lies that anyone ever heard, and so extricate myself from this danger.*

PART V

Reynard the Fox bamboozles and distracts the court with elaborate stories of nonexistent precious objects

32

The fox subtly proves himself innocent of the death of Cuwaert the Hare and of all the other charges laid against him. With flattery he regains the King's goodwill

Then spoke Reynard the Fox. "Oh, dear, are you telling me that Cuwaert is dead? Then where is Bellin the Ram? What did he bring you on his return? I gave him three jewels—I'd love to know what became of them. He should have given one of them to you, my lord the King, and the other to my lady the Queen."

The King said: "Bellin brought us nothing but Cuwaert's head, as I told you earlier, for which I took vengeance by killing him. The despicable wretch told me that he'd composed the letters in the pouch himself."

"Ah, my lord, is this the way it's turned out? I curse my birth, wretch that I am! My heart will break for sorrow now that these jewels are lost. I'm sorry to be alive. What will my wife say when she hears this? She'll go crazy with grief! As long as I live she'll never trust me again—she'll be utterly depressed when she hears this news."

The she-ape then said: "Reynard, dear nephew, what do you gain from all this grief? Let it go. Tell us instead about these jewels. Perhaps we'll work out a way to regain them if they're to be found anywhere. Master Akern will ferret them out with his book-knowledge, and we'll arrange for a curse to be pronounced in all the churches until we know where they are. They might not be lost."

"No, aunt, don't start thinking thoughts such as these, for those who've got the jewels won't easily let them go. Never did a King bestow jewels like these ones. You've nonetheless eased my heart and lifted my spirits a bit. Dear me—we can see from this how we can be deceived by the very people we most trust. Even if I have to travel the world and risk my life for it, I'll discover what happened to those jewels."

With deceptive and sorrowful words the fox said: "All my kin and friends, listen! I'll tell you what these jewels were. You'll be able to see what a great loss I've suffered.

"One of them was a ring of fine gold. Within the ring, on the finger side, there were written letters, enameled with black and blue, and there were three Hebrew names, which I was unable to decipher, since I don't read that language. There's a wise man—Master Abrion of Trier. He understands all languages and the power of all kinds of herbs. There's no animal so fierce or strong that he can't master—let him see any animal once and he'll do what he wants with it. And yet he doesn't believe in God, because he's a Jew.[36] He's the most skillful man alive, who knows the power of stones. I once showed him the ring, and he said that the names were the three names that Seth brought out of

36 An ignorantly worded statement, since of course Jews believe in God.

Paradise when he brought the oil of mercy to his father Adam. Whosoever bears these three names on his person will never be hurt by thunder or lightning. Nor will any witchcraft have power over him, and he won't be tempted to commit any sin. Neither will he receive any harm from cold, even if he were to sleep three long winter's nights in a field, and even if it snowed or froze in a storm. Master Abrion confirms that the power of these words is that strong.

"On the outer side of the ring stood a stone of three distinct colors, one part of which was crystalline red, and shone as if it had fire in it. If you traveled at night you wouldn't need any other light, because the brilliance of the stone gave out a midday intensity. The other part of the stone was as white and clear as if it'd been burnished. Whoever had any eye pain, or any swelling or headache, or any external sickness whatever, needed only wipe the affected place with this stone and he'd be immediately cured. If any man were ill through venom, or were to have poisoning through colic, swelling of the glands, kidney stone, fistula, or cancer, or any other sickness whatsoever except death itself, then all he had to do was simply to put this stone in a little water, drink it, and he'd be immediately and completely cured.

"So," said the fox, "we've good reason to grieve for the loss of such a jewel! The third color was green like glass. But there were some purple sprinkles in it. The master told me truthfully that whoever wears this stone will never suffer injury inflicted by an enemy. No man, no matter how strong and courageous, could harm him. Wherever he fought he'd be victorious, whether by night or by day, as long as he continued to look at it fasting. He'd also be beloved wherever he went, and in all company, even if he'd been hated previously. If he wore the ring, his enemies would forget their anger the moment they saw him. Even if he were naked in the field of battle against a hundred armed men, he'd be courageous and escape from his assailants with honor, as long as he was a noble gentleman without any lowborn qualities. In that case the stone wouldn't have any power.

"This stone was so precious and so powerful, I judged that I wasn't myself fit to wear it. So I sent it to my dear lord the King, who is, in my judgment, the noblest creature now living, on whom all our welfare depends, and who should be preserved from all fear, constraint, and ill fortune.

"I found this ring in my father's treasure trove. In the same place, I found a mirror and a comb that my wife wished to have at all costs. A man would be amazed who saw these treasures. I sent them to my lady the Queen, because she's been good and gracious to me. The comb can't be overpraised: it's made of the bone of a pure and noble animal, called the panther, who lives between India and the earthly paradise. He is so seductively beautiful and of a color unmatched by any under heaven except by colors found in him. What's more, he has such a sweet smell that the fragrance cures all illnesses. Because of his beauty and sweet fragrance all other animals follow him, for by his fragrance they're cured of disease. The panther has a beautiful bone, broad and slender. Whenever the beast is slain, all his fragrance is preserved in this bone, which no one can ever break. It's so tough and hard that it can never rot. Nor can fire, water, or blows destroy it. And yet it's extraordinarily light. The sweet fragrance is so powerful that anyone who smells it can't be troubled by any other worldly desire, and is at the same time cured of every disease. Its wearer experiences perfect happiness.

"The comb is polished like fine silver. Its teeth are fine and straight. Between the larger teeth and the smaller you find a large space, in which many an image is subtly carved, enameled with fine gold. The space is checkered with black and silver, enameled with silver and lapis lazuli. The carved history tells the story of how Venus, Juno, and Pallas strove for the apple of gold,[37] which each of them wanted to possess. It fell to Paris to resolve the controversy: he was to award it to the most beautiful of the three.

"Paris was at that time a shepherd who guarded his father's sheep outside the walls of Troy.[38] When he had possession of the apple, Juno promised him the greatest wealth in the world if he'd judge her to have the apple. Pallas said that if she were given the apple, she would award Paris with wisdom and strength. She would make him so great a lord that he'd be victorious over all his enemies and whomever else he wished to defeat.

37 Although this version uses the Latin names of classical Roman gods, this is a reference to the classical Greek myth of the Judgment of Venus, in which the young Trojan prince Paris must choose among the goddesses Venus, Minerva, and Juno. Paris chooses the beauty of Venus over the wisdom of Minerva and the power of Juno. Paris's disastrous choice initiates the Trojan War.

38 Reynard's set of stories offer a graded spectrum of medieval literary genres, moving down the generic-social scale, as follows: the Judgment of Paris from the classical narrative of the Trojan War; the late medieval aristocratic romance of the kind exemplified by the flying wooden horse; the animal fable of the aristocratic animals the horse and the hart; the fable of the farmyard animals of the dog and the ass; a story from the Reynard epic itself, that of Reynard's father and Tybert the Cat; the Aesopian narrative of wolf and crane. Each of these narratives, from the entire gamut of improving literature, is designed to teach a moral lesson. Each is manipulated by Reynard to neutralize ethics and to escape justice. The important lesson offered by literature is not, by this account, truth, but rhetorical skill in avoiding truth.

"Venus spoke: 'What need do you have of wealth or strength? Are you not the son of Priam, and brother to Hector? They control all Asia. Are you not already one of the masters of mighty Troy? If you give the apple to me I'll reward you with the most precious treasure in all the world. I'll give you the most beautiful woman who ever drew breath. No woman shall ever be born more beautiful. You'll then be richer than rich, and rise higher than any competitors. That is the treasure that no man can praise sufficiently. Honest, beautiful, and good women can expel many of the heart's sorrows. They're modest and wise, and bring true joy and happiness to a man.'

"Paris listened to Venus, who presented him with the prospect of such joy and so beautiful a woman that he begged Venus to name the woman who was so fair and to say where she could be found.

"Venus replied: 'I'm speaking of Helen, the wife of King Menelaus of Greece. There's no woman living in the entire world who's nobler, wealthier, better-born, or wiser.'

"Paris gave the apple to Venus, and declared that she was the most beautiful. How he afterwards captured Helen with the help of Venus, and how he brought her to Troy and married her, and the great love and delightful life that they led there together, was all carved in the space of the comb—each episode by itself, and the story written as well.

"Now I'll tell you about the mirror. The mirror's glass was so powerful that men could see in it everything that was being done either by men or beasts for a mile around. You could see everything you wanted to know. Whenever a man looked in the mirror, if he had any disease, such as stabbing eye pain or seeing

“The mirror’s glass was so powerful that men could see in it everything done by men or beasts for a mile around.”

stars, or cataracts in his eyes, then he'd be immediately healed of that complaint, such was the mighty power of the mirror.

"Is it, then, any wonder that I should be upset and angry to lose jewels of this kind? The wood in which this mirror stood was light and had been well rooted. It was called Cetine. It remains hard forever before it rots, or before worms can damage it. For that reason King Solomon sealed the interior of his temple with the same wood. Men value it dearer than fine gold. It's similar to the wood of ebony, of which King Crompart made his wooden horse for the love of King Morcadigas's daughter, who was so beautiful, and whom he thought to have won.[39] The workings of that horse were such that whoever rode it would be a hundred miles away within an hour.

"This was proven in the following way. Cleomedes, the King's son, refused to believe that the wooden horse possessed such strength and capacity. Cleomedes was young, energetic, and courageous, and wished to perform great deeds of valor to achieve worldly renown. So he leapt on the wooden horse, turned a pin on its breast, and the horse immediately flew up and left through the window. Before one could say the Lord's Prayer, Cleomedes had traveled more than ten miles. Cleomedes was terribly afraid and thought he'd never return, as the story tells more plainly. But of his fear and how far he rode on that horse of ebony wood before he mastered the skill of turning him, and how joyful he was when he understood it, and how the court was worried for him, and how he understood all this, and how he managed to return home—all this I leave aside for fear of losing time.

39 Reynard's imagined narrative is clearly a romance of the kind popular in the Burgundian court in the later Middle Ages. This story is not otherwise known.

"But all this happened by virtue of the wood, which had been used for the frame of the mirror. It was a foot wide and surrounded the mirror, in which were some strange stories illustrated with gold, black, silver, yellow, deep blue, and vermilion. These six colors were used in the illustrations to just the right degree, and under every pictured story enameled words were engraved, so that everyone could understand what each story was. By my reckoning there was never so costly, so delightful, or so beautiful a mirror.

"In the beginning of these stories was the tale of a strong and sturdy horse, which was envious of a hart that ran so far and so swiftly ahead that the horse was angry to be left so far behind, unable to catch up. He thought he'd capture and overcome the hart, no matter how much he'd suffer in doing so. So the horse spoke to a herdsman: 'If you could catch a hart that I can point out to you, I'd repay you handsomely. You'd be able to sell his horns, his hide, and his flesh.'

"The herdsman said: 'How can I meet this hart?'

"The horse said: 'Sit on me and I'll carry you. We'll hunt him until he's captured.'

"The herdsman sprang up onto the horse and, seeing the hart, rode after him, but the hart was swift and outran the horse. They hunted him so far that the horse was exhausted and said to the herdsman who rode him: 'Now dismount—I'll take a rest. I'm exhausted, and need to take a break.'

"The herdsman said: 'Think again. You're now under arrest. You can't escape me. I've got a bridle on your head and spurs on my heels, which you'll forever regret. I'll master and subdue you even if you'd sworn the contrary.'

"See how the horse brought himself into servitude and was

trapped in his own net. How easily one is caught by one's envy—the horse allowed himself to be taken and ridden. There are many who work to inflict damage on others, when they end up damaging no one but themselves.

"On that mirror one can also find the story of the ass and the dog, who both dwelt with a rich man. The man loved the dog very much, for he played with him as men do with dogs. The dog leapt up and wagged his tail and licked his master's face. Bowdewyn the Ass observed all this and with intense envy, saying to himself: 'How can this be? What can my lord see in this disgusting dog, whom I never see doing anything useful except jumping up on the master and kissing him? I, by contrast, work incessantly, carting and dragging, and doing more in a week than he, along with fifteen other dogs, does in a whole year. And yet look at him—sitting by the master at the table, and eating the flesh on bones and the big helpings, while I eat nothing but thistles and nettles, and I lie at night on the hard ground and endure many insults. I'm not going to put up with this anymore! I must work out a way of attracting the master's love and friendship just as the dog does.'

"So along came the lord, and the ass lifted up his tail and sprang with his forefeet onto the lord's shoulders. He stuck his tongue out with his eyes closed and sang, and with his feet embraced the lord around his ears. He stuck his mouth forward as if he would kiss the lord's mouth, just like the dog.

"The terrified lord cried: 'Help, help—this ass will kill me!' His servants rushed out with staves and beat the ass so hard that he thought he was going to die. So he returned to his stable and ate thistles and nettles and remained an ass just as he'd been before.

"Likewise, whoever is envious of another's good fortune

deserves to be treated in exactly the same way. So everyone agrees that the ass will eat thistles and nettles and carry heavy burdens. Even if one did pay him respect, he'd be incapable of recognizing it, but must remain stuck forever in his inveterate ways. Where asses get lordships, we seldom see good rule. They pursue nothing but their own selfish interests, yet—more's the pity—they are promoted and rise.

"Listen further: my father and Tybert the Cat went together, and swore that they'd never separate, in good times and bad. Whatever they got, they'd divide it half and half. They saw hunters coming over the field with many hounds. They leapt and ran quickly away from them as if they were afraid of being killed.

" 'Tybert,' said the fox, 'where's the best place to run to—the hunters have seen us. Do you know how we can save ourselves?' My father trusted in the promise that each had made to the other, and wouldn't, regardless of the danger, abandon Tybert.

" 'Tybert,' he said, 'I have a bag of tricks if we need it. As long as we stay together we needn't be afraid of the hunters or their dogs.'

"Tybert began to pant in terror. He said: 'Reynard, what use are words? I know only one trick, and must use it.' So he climbed high up a tree into the topmost branches under the leaves, where neither hunter nor hounds could harm him. He left my father all alone in mortal danger. The hunters set their hounds on him as energetically as they could. Men blew horns and shouted and hallowed: 'Catch and kill the fox!'

"When Tybert the Cat saw this, he mocked and jeered at my father and said: 'Cousin Reynard, now's the time to open up your bag of tricks: if you're so clever, I suggest you help yourself. You're in a fix, buddy.'

"My father was forced to endure this mockery from the very one he most trusted. He was almost captured and so was close to death. He fled in mortal fear, and let his bag slide off in order to be lighter. But that was of no use, for the dogs were swift and would have bitten him. By a stroke of luck he found an old hole, into which he crept, and so escaped the hunters and their hounds.

"So it was that this liar Tybert held his word. How many are there nowadays who don't keep their promise, and don't give a fig for breaking it? I hate Tybert for this, and it's no wonder that I hate him truly, because I love my soul too much. If saw him in danger and suffering either in body or property, I don't believe I'd care as much as I would if it were someone else suffering. I'll nonetheless neither hate nor envy him. I will, for the love of God, forgive him, despite the fact that the matter sits heavy on my soul. There's a residue of ill will, when I remember this. And why? My baser feelings rebel against my reason.

"That mirror also contained the story of how the wolf once found a dead horse, skinned on the heath. All the flesh had been eaten, but he went and bit great chunks out of the bones. He was so hungry that one of the bones got very painfully stuck sideways in his mouth. In fear for his life, he sought all the wise masters of medicine and surgeons, promising great gifts if they would cure him of this distress. At last, when he could find no remedy, he came to the crane, with his long neck and beak. The wolf asked the crane to help him out, promising that he would love and reward him so well that he'd be better off ever afterwards. The crane was impressed by the thought of the reward, and so put his head into the wolf's throat and extracted the bone with his beak. The wolf jumped aside as the bone was being extracted and cried out: 'Hey! You're hurting me! But I forgive you as long as you don't do it again. I wouldn't take that from anyone else.'

"The crane answered: 'Sir Isengrim, go and be happy, for you're restored to perfect health. Now give me what you promised.'

"The wolf said: 'Just listen to this guy! *I'm* the one who's suffered and have cause to complain, and he wants *me* to pay *him*! Not a word of thanks for the kindness I did when he put his head in my mouth and I allowed him to extract the bone without hurting him at all. What's more, he hurt me. If anyone here deserves a reward, by rights it's me!'

"This is how the cruel now thank the kindly do-gooders. When the false and wily are promoted, then respect and common profit go out the window. There are many who ought to reward and repay those who have helped them in their need, but who now find reasons not to do so, saying that *they* are the ones who've suffered and deserve amends themselves. Thus it's said—and never a truer word—let the one who chides and punishes be sure that he is himself in the clear.

"All this and much more than I can easily remember was worked into this mirror. The master who worked it was skillful in many disciplines. These jewels were far too precious for me to keep for myself, so I sent them to my dear lord the King and the Queen present here now. Where can you find people these days who give such presents to their lords? My two children were sorrowful when I sent the mirror away, for they'd taken to looking at themselves in the mirror to see how their clothing suited them perfectly.

"Ah! I had no idea that Cuwaert the Hare was so near death when I entrusted the pouch with the treasures in it to him! I had no idea to whom I might have entrusted it more safely, even if it should have cost me my life. Cuwaert and Bellin were, after all, two of my best friends.

"Grief! I denounce the murderer! I'll find out who it was, even if I have to search for him out throughout the entire world. Murder will out! Perhaps the one who knows what became of Cuwaert is in this very company here now, even if he won't declare himself. For there are many felons who mix with the honest. No man can defend himself from the wicked, since they know their business so well and can so cunningly disguise their treachery."

PART VI

Reynard aims further stories against his enemies at court, and so escapes from all charges

33

Reynard's story of his father's medicinal skill in the service of the King, and other stories targeted at Isengrim the Wolf[40]

"What astonishes me more than anything, however, is that my lord the King should so cruelly say that neither I nor my father ever served him well. That a King should say that just stuns me, but so many things come to his notice that he forgets one service and another. So it goes with me.

"Dear lord, can't you remember when my lord your father was still alive, and you were a young one of no more than two years? My father came from the university in Montpellier, where he'd studied medicinal therapies for five years. He'd learned how to diagnose from urine as well as he knew the back of his hand. He also knew the properties of herbs—which of them were vicious, and which were laxatives. He was a distinguished master in that science—in fact he could well have worn the cloth of silk and a golden belt.[41]

"When he came to court he found the King in a great sick-

40 In order better to clarify the structure of the narrative, I have introduced a new chapter to Caxton's chapter division here.

41 Almost certainly the garb of the late medieval doctor.

ness, which pained him sorely, because he loved the King above all other lords. The King wouldn't dispense with him, and when he arrived everyone else had permission to leave. Your father trusted none so much as my father.

"He said: 'Reynard, I'm ill, and it's getting worse.'

"My father replied: 'My dear lord, here's a bowl. Urinate in it, and as soon as I see it I'll be able to diagnose what your malady is and also how you'll be cured.'

"The King did as my father advised, for he trusted no living person more. It's true that my father acted badly towards you, but his betrayal was prompted by evil and malevolent beasts. I was amazed at the whole story, but the rebellion happened near the time of his death.

"My father said: 'My lord, if you wish to be cured, you must eat the liver of a wolf who's at least seven years old. You must on no account forgo this cure. If you do, you'll die. Your urine shows it plainly.'

"The wolf stood right there beside the King, and said nothing. But the King said to him: 'Sir Isengrim, you've heard that I must have your liver if I'm to be cured.'

"The wolf then answered: 'No, my lord. Not so! I know well that I am not yet five years old—I've heard my mother say so.'

"My father said: 'What does it matter what Isengrim says? Let him be cut open and I'll be able to tell from the liver whether or not it'll be good for you.'

"So the wolf was taken off to the kitchen and his liver was cut out. The King ate it and was entirely cured of his sickness. He then thanked my father profusely, and commanded all his household, on peril of their lives, that from then on they must all call my father 'Master Reynard.'

"My father remained with the King, and was trusted in all

"My lord, if you wish to be cured, you must eat the liver of a wolf at least seven years old."

things. He was always required to be at the King's side. The King gave him a garland of roses, which he had to wear on his head at all times. But now everything is topsy-turvy! All the good things that he did are forgotten. Instead, these voracious and rapacious felons are promoted and set on the high bench, where they're heard and treated as the great. Wise folks are set back. And true lords are the ones who lose out. For when a covetous man of low birth is made a lord and promoted to great rank and power above his neighbors, then he forgets himself and where he came from. He has no pity for any man's pain, and neither does he hear anyone's petition uness he first receives great gifts. His only intent and desire is to amass goods and to become yet more powerful.

"Oh, how many greedy men now populate the courts of lords! They flatter and grovel. They're obsequious to the prince only for their selfish advantage. If, however, the prince needs them or their goods, they'd sooner let him die or suffer badly before they'd give or lend him a thing. They're like the wolf, who'd have preferred the King to die than to give him his own liver. As for me, I'd rather twenty such wolves died before the King or the Queen would suffer. The loss of wolves would be of least account.

"My lord, all this occurred in your youth. I suppose you've forgotten my father's service. I have also served you with reverence, honor, and courtesy. Let this be, even though you repay me with small thanks for it now. Perhaps you've also forgotten what I'm about to say. And I say it not so as to blame you in any way—since you are worthy of all the honor and reverence that any man could give. You possess that by the inheritance of your noble progenitors, on accout of which I, your humble subject and servant, am bound to perform every service I can for you.

"It happened once that I was walking with Isengrim the Wolf. We'd both subdued a swine. Because of his noisy squealing we bit him to death. You, sire, came from afar out of a grove. You greeted us affably and declared us welcome. You also declared that you and my lady the Queen, who followed you, were especially hungry, and had nothing to eat. You asked us to give you a portion of our winnings. Isengrim replied with so little enthusiasm that a man could hardly hear him. I, on the contrary, spoke up and said: 'Yes, my lord, with pleasure! We only wish it were a larger portion, and we're delighted that you should have a part.'

"The wolf then moved off a little, as he always does. As he moved, he took half for himself, and he gave you and the Queen a quarter. As for the remaining quarter, he swallowed it as quickly as he could, because in fact he wanted to eat it all himself. He gave me just half the lungs. I pray to God that he might suffer for that. Thus he revealed his true nature.

"Before men could have sung the Creed, you, my lord, had eaten your part. And yet you wanted more, since you weren't full. And because Isengrim didn't offer you any more, you lifted your right foot and hit him between the ears so that you tore the skin above his eyes. He couldn't endure that, but he bled and howled and ran away, leaving his part of the spoils behind.

"You then said to him: 'Hurry back here and bring us more. And from now on, look to it that you make a better division.'

"I said: 'My lord, if it pleases you I'll go with him. I understand very well what you've said.'

"I went with Isengrim. He was bleeding and groaning only softly, despite his pain—he didn't dare cry out loudly. We hunted so actively that we brought a calf back. And when you saw us come with it, you laughed for joy. You told me that I was a swift hunter. 'I see that you can find prey well when you take charge of the business. You're just the person to send in need. The calf is good and fat. You divide it up.'

" 'My lord,' I said, 'with pleasure. You get half. The other half is for my lady the Queen. The sweetbread, liver, lungs, and the innards go to your children. Isengrim the Wolf gets the head, and I'll take the feet.'

"Then you replied: 'Reynard, who taught you to make so courteous a division?'

" 'My lord, the priest here—the one sitting beside us with the bloody crown, who lost his skin after his discourteous division of the swine—it was he who taught me. For his greed and rapacity, he got nothing but injury and shame. Oh, dear, there are so many wolves these days, who unjustly destroy and consume anyone they can subdue. They spare neither flesh nor blood, friend nor foe: whatever they can get, they eat. Woe to the land and to the towns where the wolves are in power!'

"My lord: I served you in that instance, and in many others I could recount were it not so time-consuming, despite the fact that, from what you say, you seem to remember very little. If you'd survey your kingdom well, you wouldn't speak as you do.

"I remember the days when no great matter would be decided in this court without consulting me. Although the present matter has fallen out as it has, it may well be the case that once again my words will be heard and trusted as well as those of others, always within the bounds of justice. For I have no desire to exceed those bounds.

"If there are any here who can say and prove by reliable witnesses that I committed a crime, then I submit myself willingly to due process of law. And if anyone lays charges for which he can produce no witnesses, then let me be judged by the law and custom of this court."

The King then said: "Reynard, your argument that the only thing I know about Cuwaert's death is that Bellin the Ram brought his head here in the pouch is strong. I therefore release you in complete freedom, since there's no witness to any crime."

"My dear lord," Reynard replied, "may God surely thank you! You've made the right decision, for his death makes me so sad—I think my heart will break in two. When they left, my heart was so heavy that I was about to faint. I now know that it was a foreboding of the loss that was then so close upon me."

Most of those who were there in court and who listened to the fox's story of the jewels and how he made his case and defended himself supposed that none of it was made up, and that he was telling the truth. They pitied him for his loss and grief. The King and the Queen both pitied him. They counseled him not to grieve overmuch.

They also suggested that he set himself to look for the jewels, given that he'd praised them so much. It was also true that the King and Queen had an intense desire to possess those jewels, because Reynard had told them that he had sent the treasure to them. Though they had never received them, they nonetheless thanked him. And they directed him to offer his help in the finding of the jewels.

The fox understood what they meant perfectly well. His thoughts on their account were no better for that.

He said: "May God thank you, my lord and my lady the Queen, who offer such kindly comfort to me in my grief. Neither I nor any of my supporters will rest, night or day. I'll run and I'll pray, I'll threaten and beg in all the four corners of the world, even if I look forever, until I know what became of them. And I pray my lord the King that, if they're in such a place where I wouldn't be able to retrieve them by prayer, strength, or entreaty, you'll help and continue to offer your support. For the matter concerns you, and the property is yours. Further, it's your responsibility to enact justice for theft and murder, which are both part of this case."

"Reynard," said the King, "I won't fail in that responsibility once you know where the jewels are. You always have my support."

"Oh, dear lord, you give me too much. If I had the power and the strength, I'd repay you."

Now the fox had his master firmly where he wanted him, for he had the King eating out of his paw, just as he wanted. He considered his position unexpectedly advantageous. He'd concocted so many lies that he could move freely wherever he wanted, without anyone objecting. Anyone, that is, except Isengrim, who was angry and upset.

Isengrim said: "Oh, noble King, are you so childish as to believe this false and subtle felon? Will you allow yourself to be deceived in this way? If I were in charge, I'd take longer to believe him, for he's entirely wrapped in murder and treason. He's mocking you to your face. I'll tell you another story. I'm glad to see him here now. All his lies won't help him once I'm done with him."

PART VII

Final combats between Isengrim the Wolf and Reynard the Fox, from which Reynard emerges victorious

34

Isengrim the Wolf accuses the fox

"y lord, I ask you to listen carefully. This treacherous thief betrayed my wife once in the most disgraceful and dishonest way. It happened on a winter's day that they traveled together by a great lake. He made my wife believe that he'd teach her to catch fish with her tail. All she had to do was let it hang in the water for a good while. So many fish would then cleave to it that four wolves wouldn't be able to eat them all. My foolish wife supposed that he was telling the truth. So she went into the mud up to her belly before she came to the water. And when she was in the deepest part of the water, he told her to hold the tail still until the fish came.

"She held the tail so long that it was frozen hard in the ice and she was unable to pull it out. When Reynard saw this, he sprang up onto her body. I swear it! He had his way with her there and forced himself on her so disgracefully that I'm ashamed to tell the story. She was unable to protect herself, the poor animal, so deep did she stand in the mud. Reynard can't deny this, for I found him *in flagrante delicto.* I happened to be walking on the bank, and I could see him on my wife, shoving and sticking as men do when they're at such work and play. What grief I suffered

“I happened to be walking on the bank.”

in my heart! I almost fainted, and cried, insofar as I was able, 'Reynard, what are you doing there?'

"When he spotted me so close, he jumped off and went on his way. I approached my wife in great distress. I went deep into the mud and water before I could break the ice. She endured intense pain before she could extract her tail, and even then she left a bit of the tail behind. We were likely to have lost both our lives there, because she was sobbing and crying so loudly from the pain that men of the village came out with staves and swords, with flails and pitchforks. And the women came with their spinning poles and shouted pitilessly: 'Kill them! kill them!' and they struck us viciously. Never in my life was I so afraid.

"We barely escaped. We ran until we were sweating. There was a peasant who hit us with a pike that hurt us so much, given his strength and rapidity. If it hadn't been night, we'd surely have been killed. The foul old women would've happily beaten us. They said we'd bitten their sheep. They cursed us foully. Then we entered a field full of broom and brambles and hid ourselves from the peasants, who didn't dare pursue us further at night, but turned back for home. So consider this disgraceful business, my lord: this is murder, rape, and treason, for which justice should be executed with rigor."

Reynard answered: "If this were true, it would profoundly impugn my honor and reputation! God forbid that it be proved!

"Now, it is true that I did teach Isengrim's wife how she should catch fish in a place, and I also showed her a good way of crossing into the water without passing through the mud. But she ran so rashly when she heard the word 'fish' that she wouldn't hold to any track, but went directly into the ice, in which she was frozen. And that was because she waited for too long. She would've had plenty of fish if only she'd have been happy with enough. It often happens that the person who wants everything loses everything. Being overgreedy was never a good idea. For an animal can't be satisfied.

"And when I saw her stuck in the ice, I wanted to help her, so I heaved and I shoved and I pushed her this way and that, but it was useless: she was too heavy for me. Then Isengrim arrived and saw how I shoved and pushed and did my best. He, disgraceful lowlife that he is, foully slandered me with his ribald nonsense, just as no-gooders always do.

"But, my dear lord, it was nothing of the kind. He's spreading lies about me with treacherous intent. Perhaps his eyes were dazzled as he looked from above. He cried and cursed me and swore many oaths that I'd pay for it. When I heard him curse and threaten, I immediately left him at it until he exhausted himself. He then went and heaved and shoved and helped his wife out, before leaping and running with her to get warm, or else they'd have died in the cold.

"Everything I've said is the whole truth: I wouldn't lie once to you for a thousand marks of fine gold. That would ill-become me, and whatever happens to me, I'll tell the truth, just as my elders have always done since the time we reached the age of reason. If you're in any doubt that anything whatsoever I've said is true, then give me respite of eight days for me to take counsel. I'll bring you such information, with wholly reliable evidence, that you and your council will always trust me from now on.

"My relations with the wolf have been clearly announced here: he's a malicious and immoral scoundrel, as was demonstrated when he divided up the swine. So now you can see by his own words that he's a terrible slanderer of women—now everyone can see it. Who would want to play such tricks on so steadfast a wife when she was about to die? Now ask his wife if it's as he says it is. If she tells the truth, I know that her story will square with mine."

Then spoke Arswind, the wife of Isengrim the Wolf: "Ah, cruel Reynard, no one can protect himself from you, since you're so eloquent. You disguise your treachery and treason so well, but in the end you'll be punished. How did you bring me once into the well? There were the two buckets hanging by one cord running through one pulley, where one bucket went up as the other went down. You sat in one bucket down in the well, terribly afraid. I came along and heard you sighing in your suffering and asked how you got down there. You replied that you'd eaten so many fish in the well's water that your stomach was about to burst. I said: 'Tell me how I can join you.' To which you replied: 'Aunt, just jump into the bucket hanging there and you'll be with me in a jiffy.'

"So I jumped in and down I went, while you came up. I was furious, but you said: 'So it goes in the world: up comes one as another goes down.' Then you sprang out and went your way, leaving me sitting there alone, sitting for a whole day hungry and cold. I endured many a blow before I could escape."

"Aunt," said the fox, "though the strokes hurt you, I'd rather they fell on you than me, for you're better able to bear strokes than I. For one of us had to be beaten. I gave you a good lesson, if you were capable of learning it. So reflect on it, and next time don't be rash in believing everything someone tells you, even if he's a friend or cousin. For every man seeks his own advantage. Whoever fails to weigh words is a fool, especially when they're in danger of their life."

35

A fair parable of the fox and the wolf

"y lord," said Arswind, "just listen to the way he can blow with every wind, and how gracefully he presents his cases."

"He has often brought me into harm and hurt in this way," said the wolf. "He once betrayed me to my aunt the she-ape when I was very afraid, for I almost left one of my ears there. If the fox will tell the story, I'll give him the first part of it, for I can't tell it so well. But he'll criticize me."

"Well," said the fox, "I'll tell it without stammering. I'll say nothing but the truth, and I ask that you listen carefully.

"Isengrim came into the wood and complained to me that he was especially hungry. I never saw him not hungry, not even when he was completely full. I can't think where the food he consumes goes. I see even now by his face that hunger is making him grimace.

"When I heard him complain, I pitied him, and told him that I was hungry too. So the wolf and I traveled together half a day and didn't find a thing. Then Isengrim started whining, crying that he couldn't take another step. I then spotted a great hole in the middle of a hedge's foliage thick with brambles. I heard a rushing sound from within it, but had no idea what it was. So I said: 'Go in and see if there's anything there for us; I know there's something.'

"Then he said: 'Cousin, I wouldn't creep into that hole for twenty pounds, without first knowing what's inside it. It strikes me that there's something dangerous in there. I'll wait here under this tree, if you'll go in first. But be sure to return immediately and tell me what's in there. You know many tricks and can look after yourself much better than I can.'

"So you can already see, my lord the King, that he made a weak creature take on the danger, while he—the great, tall, strong one—waited outside and rested himself at his leisure. See if I didn't do him a good turn in there.

"I wouldn't willingly endure the fear again that I suffered there for all the wealth in the world, unless I knew how to escape. But I went in courageously, where I found the passage dark, long, and broad. Before I came fully into the hole, I saw a powerful light that came in from one side. There lay a great ape with two wide eyes, which glimmered like fire. She had a huge mouth with long teeth, and sharp nails on both feet and hands. I thought it was a polecat, a baboon, or a monkey, for I never saw a more disgusting animal. Three of her children lay beside her, who were no less repulsive, for they resembled their mother. When they saw me coming they gaped at me and fell completely silent. I was afraid, and wanted to get out of there, but I thought to myself, *I'm in here and I must get through this as best I can.*

"As I looked at her, it seemed to me that she was bigger than Isengrim the Wolf; and her children were bigger than I was. Never did I see an uglier household. They lay on dirty hay that was saturated with their own pee. They were slimed and clotted to their ears in their own dung. It stank so much that I almost suffocated.

"I didn't dare say anything but compliments, so I said: 'Aunt, may God give you a good day, and all my cousins your beautiful children—they are the handsomest young ones for their age that I ever saw. Oh, Lord God, how well they please me. How lovely and pretty each one of them is! For beauty alone they could be the children of a great King. By rights we ought to thank you for enlarging our lineage in this way. Dear aunt, when I heard that you'd given birth, I couldn't wait at home, but felt compelled to pay you a courtesy call. I'm only sorry that I hadn't heard the news earlier.'

" 'Reynard, cousin,' she said, 'you're very welcome. I'm grateful that you've found me and come to see me. Dear cousin, you're loyal, and everyone calls you wise. You also promote the interests of your kin with great honor. You must teach my children some wisdom, so that they know what they should and shouldn't do. I've thought about you, because you prosper by keeping company with the good.'

"Oh, how well pleased I was when I heard these words. I had this in mind at the start when I called her 'aunt,' even though she was no relation to me whatsoever. For my real aunt is Dame Rukenawe, standing over there, who has a habit of producing wise children.

"I said: 'Aunt, my life and my property are at your disposal. Whatever I can do for you, by night and day, I'll gladly teach your children as best I can.' In fact I wanted nothing more than to be away, because of the stink, and also because I was worried about Isengrim, who was hungry.

"So I said: 'I entrust you and your pretty children, dear aunt, to God, and take my leave for the moment. My wife will be regretting my long absence.'

"'Dear cousin, you won't leave until you've eaten, for if you did I'd think you ill-mannered.' Then she stood up and took me into another hole, where there was so much food of harts and hinds, roes, pheasants, partridges, and other meats that I couldn't understand where all this food came from. When I'd eaten my bellyful, she gave me a great chunk of hind to eat with my wife and family when I got home. I was ashamed to take it, but I couldn't do otherwise. So I thanked her and took my leave. She asked me to come again soon, and I said I would. And so I left, happy that everything had gone off so well.

"I rushed out, and saw Isengrim groaning on the ground. I asked him how he was, to which he replied: 'Never worse! It's a miracle I'm alive! Have you brought any food to eat? I'm dying of hunger!'

"I pitied him and gave all that I had, and in doing so saved his life, for which he thanked me profusely, even though he repays me now with malevolence.

"He devoured the food immediately, and said: 'Reynard, dear cousin, what did you find in that hole? I'm hungrier now than I was before. My teeth have now been whetted for a good meal.'

"I replied: 'Uncle, go quickly and easily into that hole. You'll find plenty. My aunt is lying there with her children. If you'll be economical with the truth and tell some whoppers, you'll have all you want. If, though, you tell the truth, you'll suffer.'

"My lord, wasn't this sufficiently forewarned, to whomever would understand it? All he had to do was say the opposite of all he thought. But ill-mannered and gross animals are incapable of understanding wise counsel. That's why they hate subtle devices, because they can't invent them themselves. All the same, he said he'd go in and tell as many lies as he'd need to before anything went wrong—he'd tell so many that men would be amazed.

"And so off he went into that stinking hole and found the ape there. She resembled the devil's daughter. Horrible filth, congealed in gobbets, hung on her children. Then Isengrim cried out: 'Ugh! These horrid urchins disgust me! They come directly out of hell. Men could use them to frighten devils! Go and drown them—I hope they suffer bad fortune! Never have I set eyes on more disgusting vermin. They make my hair stand on end!'

" 'Sir Isengrim,' she said, 'what can I do about it? They're my children. I must be mother to them. What is it to you if they be ugly or handsome? They cost you nothing. We had a guest earlier, better and wiser than you, who's a close cousin to them. He said that they were pretty. Who sent you here with your bad manners?'

" 'Dame, if you want to know, I'm interested in your food. It's better given to me than to these disgusting brats.'

"She said, 'There's no food here.'

" 'Oh, yes, there is,' he replied.

"And with that he went headlong towards the food and was about to go into the hole where it was. But my aunt jumped up with her children and they ran at him so fiercely with their sharp, long nails that the blood ran over his eyes. I heard him cry out in pain and howl, but as far as I know he didn't put up a fight. Instead, he ran out of the hole, scratched and bitten, with his coat and skin torn all over. His face was covered with blood and he'd almost lost an ear.

"He groaned and poured out his troubles to me. I asked him if he'd lied well, to which he replied: 'I said as I saw: she was a disgusting bitch with hideous brats.'

"'No, uncle,' said I, 'you ought to have said it like this: "Fair niece, how are you and your pretty children, my well-loved cousins, getting on?"'

"The wolf said: 'I'd much rather be hanged than say that.'

"'And so, uncle, you must receive such payment in return. Occasionally it's smarter to lie than to say the truth. Those who are better, wiser, and stronger than we are have done so before us.'

"And so you see, my lord King, how the wolf got his red cap. Now he stands before us simply, as if he were completely innocent. Pray ask him if it wasn't as I tell it. If I'm not mistaken, my story was pretty accurate."

36

Isengrim presents his glove to the fox as a challenge to fight

he wolf replied: "I can put up with your mockery and scorn, along with your cruel and venomous words, you outright thief. You said that I was almost dead for hunger when you helped me in my need. That's a barefaced lie: you gave me a bone after you'd eaten all the flesh on it. And you mock me by saying that I'm hungry right now. That's an insult to my honor. How many humiliating insults have you uttered with your treacherous lies! And you say that I conspired for the King's death in order to get the treasure that you say is in Hulsterloe. And you have also shamed and slandered my wife, so much that she'll never recover. If I didn't avenge this, I'd be shamed forever afterwards!

"I've put up with you for far too long, but now you won't escape me. I can't prove my story, but I declare before my lord and before everyone present that you're a false traitor and a murderer. I'll prove this and make it good on your body. Only then will our dispute be resolved. That's why I'm casting my glove at you. You have to take it up. I'll get justice from you or die in the attempt."

Reynard the Fox thought to himself: *How did I end up courting a fight? We're ill-matched. I won't be able to oppose this strong thief. All my legal argument has come to nothing.*

37

Reynard the Fox takes up the glove, and the King sets a day for their combat

et, thought the fox, *I do have one advantage. The claws of his feet have been removed, when he was unshod for my sake, and his feet are still painful. He'll be a bit weaker.*

The fox stated indignantly: "Whoever calls me a traitor or a murderer is a plain liar! And especially you, Isengrim! You've brought me where I have long wanted to be. Look: here's my pledge that you're telling nothing but lies, and that I'll defend myself and prove you're a liar."

The King received the pledges and allowed the combat. He demanded the backup teams for the combatants to confirm that both would present for combat on the following day, as they were now required to do. The bear and the cat stood as support team for the wolf. Grimbart the Badger and Byteluys the Ape stood for the fox.

38

Rukenawe the She-Ape gives Reynard tactical coaching for his fight with Isengrim the Wolf

The she-ape said to the fox: "Nephew Reynard, listen to my advice about this fight. Stay cool and be smart. Your uncle once taught me a prayer that works for those about to fight. A great master and a wise scholar, the Abbot of Boudelo,[42] taught him. He said that whosoever says this prayer devoutly will not be beaten in battle that day. Therefore, dear nephew, don't be afraid. I'll read it to you tomorrow morning. You'll then be certain to beat the wolf. It's better to fight than to hang."

"Thanks, dear aunt," said the fox. "The dispute I've taken on is just, and so I hope I'll succeed. Your prayer will be a big help."

All his kin stayed by him all night, to help him get through the night. His aunt Dame Rukenawe the She-Ape constantly pondered on his advantages. She had all his hair from head to tail shaved off. She greased his entire body with olive oil, so that it was so oily and slippery that the wolf wouldn't be able to get a grip on him.

42 A wholly invented figure.

She said: "Dear cousin, you must drink as much as you can to have plenty of urine for tomorrow. But don't expel it until you come to the fight. When the moment comes, you'll piss a bellyful into your rough tail, and smack the wolf right in his beard. If you could sock him directly in the eyes you'll deprive him of his sight, and that will set him at a big disadvantage. Otherwise, be sure to hold your tail fast between your legs, so that he can't catch you with it. Also, hold your ears down flat against your head so that he can't get a grip on them. Look to your own safety, and jump from his strokes at the beginning. Let him leap and run at you, and you should run to where there's the most dust. Stir it up with your feet, so that it flies up in his eyes, which will blind him. The moment he rubs his eyes, take your chance and hit and bite him where you'll inflict the most pain. And be sure always to hit him directly in the face with your pissy tail, so he won't know where he is. And let him run after you, to exhaust him. His feet are still painful since you took his shoes. Even if he's strong, he's got no heart—that's my advice.

"Cunning is superior to strength. Therefore watch out for yourself, and put yourself in a defensive position, so that you and the rest of us can win honor from all this. I'd be sorry to see you lose. I'll teach you the words that your Uncle Mertin taught me, to overcome your enemy, as I'm sure you'll do."

With that she put her hand on his head and pronounced these words: "Blaerde, Shay, Alphenio, Kasbue, Gorfons, Alsbuifrio.[43] Nephew, now you're safe from all mischief. And fear. I suggest that you rest yourself a bit, for it'll soon be morning, and you'll be in better condition. We'll wake you in time."

"Aunt," said the fox, "I'm so happy. I hope God repays you for

43 A spell constituted of pure nonsense.

all the good you've done me. I'll never deserve it. I don't think anything can harm me, since you've said those holy words over me."

Then he went and lay down under a tree in the grass and slept until the sun had risen. The otter came and woke him and told him to get up. He gave him a good young duck to eat, saying: "Dear cousin, I've made many a dip in the water this past night before I could catch this fat young duck. I took it from a hunter. It's yours to eat."

Reynard said: "What a lovely gift! I'd be a fool to refuse it. Thanks, cousin—I'm grateful that you should think of me, and if I live I'll repay you."

The fox ate the duck without any sauce or bread. It tasted so good and went down so well. As a supplement to this meal he drank four great draughts of water. Then he went directly to battle, with his supporters on hand.

39

The fox comes into the field of combat

hen the King saw Reynard thus shorn and oiled, he said to him: "Ah, fox, how well you can look after your own interests!"

The King was surprised to see Reynard looking so ugly, but the fox remained completely silent, only kneeling down low to the earth before the King and the Queen, and then going to the field. The wolf was ready and was boasting arrogantly. The umpires of the field were the leopard and the lynx. They produced the Bible, on which the wolf swore that the fox was a traitor and a murderer, and that he was the most traitorous of all. He would prove that claim on his body and make it good. Reynard the Fox swore that the wolf was lying like a false felon and a cursed thief, and that he would prove that on the wolf's body. When this was done the umpires instructed them to do their best.

Then everyone retired to the sidelines of the field but Dame Rukenawe. She stayed by the fox and told him to remember precisely the advice that she'd given him. She said: "Remember, too, that when you were seven years old you were already clever enough to move at night without lantern or moonlight, wherever you knew there was food to be won. You're reputed among the people to be clever and subtle. Take care to operate so that you win the prize, and then you and all of us who are your friends will have the honor and praise of it forever afterwards."

He replied: "Dear aunt, I remember it very well indeed. I'll do my best and follow your wise counsel. I hope to succeed and bring honor to all my kin, and shame and confusion to my enemies."

"May God grant it you," she answered.

40

The fox and the wolf fight together

ith that she quit the field and left it to the combatants. The wolf stepped furiously to the fox and splayed his forefeet, thinking to clasp the fox in them, but the fox sprang nimbly away, because he was more agile than the wolf. The wolf leapt after the fox and pursued him mercilessly, while their friends stood on the sidelines and watched. The wolf had a broader stride than Reynard and often overtook him. He lifted his foot and would have struck him, but the fox saw it coming and hit the wolf in the face with his rough and pee-sodden tail.

The wolf thought he'd been completely blinded, the pee smarted so badly in his eyes. Reynard took his advantage and stood with the wind behind him, scratching the dust with his feet so that it flew directly up into the wolf's eyes. The wolf was so painfully blinded by this that he was obliged to abandon the chase. For the dust and the pee stuck to his eyes so painfully that he had to rub it off and wash it away. Then Reynard approached fiercely and bit the wolf hard three times on the head.

Reynard said: "What's up, Mr. Wolf? Has someone bitten you? How're things? I haven't finished with you yet. Hold on and I'll bring something new. You've stolen many lambs and destroyed many simple creatures, and now you've charged me falsely and

So began a huge battle that lasted an age.

brought me to this pass. I'm going to pay you back for all this. I've been chosen to repay you for your old sins. God won't permit your rapacity and wickedness another day. I'll absolve you, all right, and that will be good for your soul. Take the penance patiently, for your days are numbered, and hell shall be your purgatory. Your life is now at my mercy. If you come and kneel before me, asking forgiveness and acknowledging yourself beaten, I'll spare you despite the fact that you're wicked. For my conscience tells me that I shouldn't willingly kill any man."

These mocking, pitiless words almost sent Isengrim the Wolf crazy with anger. That disabled him so badly that he didn't know what to say—he was plain furious. The wounds inflicted by Reynard bled and hurt intensely. Isengrim considered how he could best avenge himself. He angrily raised his foot and hit Reynard on the head with a powerful blow, so that the fox fell. Then the wolf leapt and thought he'd captured him, but the fox was agile and wily. He recovered quickly and confronted him fiercely. So began a huge battle that lasted for an age.

The wolf hated the fox intensely, as was clear to everyone. He sprang after him ten times in a row and tried to grab him, but the fox's skin was so slippery and oily that he escaped. So subtle and fast was the fox that frequently, when the wolf thought he had him, the fox slipped between his legs and under his belly, turning again to deliver a stroke of his pissy tail in Isengrim's eyes, so that the wolf again thought he'd been blinded.

Reynard repeated this often. And whenever he'd struck such a blow, he went upwind and raised the dust, which filled Isengrim's eyes. Isengrim was nearly desperate and saw that he was at a disadvantage. Yet his strength was much greater than the fox's. Reynard took many painful blows when Isengrim could reach him. They exchanged blows and bites when they saw their chance. Each did his best to destroy the other. I wish I could have seen such a battle! One was clever and one was strong. One fought with brawn, the other with brains.

The wolf was angry that the fox could survive his attack for so long. If Isengrim's front paws had been in good shape the fox wouldn't have survived at all, but his wounds were so open he couldn't run properly. And the fox could stop and start better than he could. The fox also swung his tail into the wolf's eyes so often that the wolf thought his eyes were falling out.

At last the wolf said to himself: *I'll put an end to this fight. How long will this wretch last against me? I'm so powerful, I'd suffocate him if I pressed against him. It's shameful that I let him get away for so long. Men will mock and jeer at me because I'm losing here. I'm seriously wounded and bleeding badly. And he's drowning me with his piss, and throwing so much dust and sand in my eyes that soon I'll be blind if I let it go on. I'll take a risk and see what comes of it.*

With that he hit Reynard on the head with his foot, so that Reynard fell. Before he could get up, Isengrim caught him in his teeth and lay on him as if he would suffocate him. At this point Reynard was truly frightened, as were all his supporters when they saw him lying under the wolf. On the opposing side, Isengrim's friends rejoiced. The fox defended himself well with his claws as he lay on his back, and landed many blows. The wolf didn't dare try to inflict much harm with his feet, but snatched at Reynard with his teeth, trying to bite him. When the fox saw these bites coming his way, he was even more frightened. He hit the wolf in the head with his forefeet, and tore the skin off between his brows and his ears, so that one of his eyes hung out. This hurt the wolf badly. He howled and wept and cried loudly, making a fearful racket. His blood ran like a river.

41

Reynard the Fox, under the wolf, cleverly flatters him, so allowing Reynard to get back on top

The wolf wiped his eyes. The fox was glad when he saw that, because he wrestled so vigorously that he could jump back on his feet while the wolf was thus occupied. The wolf was upset about this, and hit him before he escaped, holding him tightly in his forearms, regardless of his own bleeding.

Reynard was now in trouble. They wrestled long and hard. The wolf grew so angry that he forgot all his pain and threw the fox flat on the ground, putting him in extreme danger. For the paw that he used to break his fall landed in Isengrim's mouth. He was afraid he might lose it.

The wolf said to the fox: "Now choose. Either acknowledge that you're beaten or else I'll kill you for sure. The scattering of the dust, your piss, your mockery, your defense, and all your tricks: none of these will help you now. You can't escape. You've done so much damage, you've inflicted so much shame on me—now I've lost one eye, I'm so badly wounded."

Reynard clearly understood his position. He had to choose

either to surrender or die. He knew the choice was crucial. He had to say one thing or the other.

He immediately settled on what he'd say, and began speaking elegantly in this way: "Dear uncle, I'll gladly become your man with all my property. For you, I'll go to the Holy Sepulcher and receive pardon and profit for your cloister from all the churches in the Holy Land. This will hugely profit both your soul and the souls of your ancestors. I don't believe that any such offer has ever been made to any King. And I'll serve you as I'd serve our Holy Father the Pope. Everything I manage will be your property, and I'll be your servant, making all my kin do likewise. You'll be a lord above lords. Who'd dare lift a finger against you? Furthermore, whatever winnings I get—poultry, geese, partridges, plovers, fish or flesh, whatever!—you, your wife, and your children will have the first pick before I take a single bite. What's more, I'll stay by your side, so that no harm will come to you wherever you are. You're strong and I'm clever. Let's stick together so that one of us supplies the ideas and the other the brute force. That way nothing can hurt us.

"We're so closely related that strictly speaking there shouldn't be any disagreement between us. I wouldn't have fought against you if I could've escaped. But you legally required me to fight, so I was forced to do what I wouldn't have done willingly. But in this battle I've been courteous to you. I've not yet shown my utmost strength, as I would've done if you weren't known to me. The nephew ought to spare the uncle. This is a good custom, and we should observe it. Dear uncle, I've now fought according to this rule. And you can be sure that I avoided wounding you as much as I could have, from the moment I ran ahead of you—my heart wouldn't permit me do otherwise. I could've hurt you much more than I did, but the thought never entered my head.

"In fact I've not hurt you or done so much damage that you've been hindered in any way, except what happened by accident to your eye. I'm very sorry about that. It pains me deeply. I wish, dear uncle, that it hadn't happened in this way, but that I'd lost my eye and that you'd been made happy by that.

"Nonetheless, you'll have a great advantage from the loss of your eye. For when you sleep from now on you need shut only one window, whereas the rest of us must shut two. My wife, children, and kin will fall down before your feet in front of the King, and in front of anyone you want them to, and they will all pray humbly that you'll allow Reynard your nephew to live. I'll also acknowledge that I've often wronged you and told lies about you. How could any lord have greater honor than what I'm offering you? I wouldn't think of doing this for anyone else. Therefore I beg you to rest content with this.

"I know you could kill me now if you wanted to. But if you did, what would you gain? You'd have to guard yourself forever afterwards against my kin and friends. It's a sign of wisdom to measure oneself in anger and not succumb to rash action, and to look ahead to what might happen afterwards. Whoever can stand back and reflect when he's angry is truly wise. There are many fools who rush in so madly in the heat of the moment that afterward they regret it, when it's too late. But uncle, you're too wise to do that. It's preferable to have reputation, honor, calm, and peace. It's also better to have many friends who stand by ready to help than to have shame, injury, and distress, along with many enemies lying in wait to inflict injury. It brings, furthermore, no honor to kill a man once you've beaten him. It's not a matter of my life—whether I live or die is of little consequence—but you'd be shamed."

Isengrim replied: "You thief, how happy you'd be to be free

and quit of me. I hear that in your speech. If you were free and on your feet, you wouldn't count me worth one eggshell. You can promise all the world to me with fine gold, but I won't let you escape. I don't give a damn for you and all your friends and kin. Everything you've said here is bunkum. Do you think you've fooled me? I've known you for a long time. I'm no bird to be trapped or taken in by husks—I know good corn when I see it. Oh, how you'd mock me if I let you escape! You might perhaps have got away with this with someone who didn't know you, but with me you're wasting your breath by buttering me up. For I see too easily through your subtle, lying tales. You've so often tricked me that I'd be a fool to trust you now.

"You false, stinking wretch, you said that you spared me in this battle. Just look at me: Haven't I lost an eye? What's more, you've wounded my head in twenty places. Not once would you let me catch my breath. I'd be a complete fool to spare you now, or to pity you, given the shame and confusion you've inflicted on me. What grieves me more than anything is that you've dishonored and slandered Arswind my wife, whom I love as my life. You've raped and deceived her, and that'll stay with me forever. As often as it comes to mind, my anger and hatred towards you renews itself."

While Isengrim was speaking, the fox was thinking hard about extricating himself. He forced his free paw between the wolf's legs and gripped the wolf hard by the balls, before twisting them so violently that the wolf howled and cried out with the intense pain. The fox was then able to withdraw his other paw from the wolf's mouth. The wolf was in such terrible pain from the tight twist the fox was applying to his balls that he spat blood and shat himself.

42

Isengrim the Wolf is beaten and the combat resolved. Reynard the Fox is the winner

he pain in Isengrim's balls was worse than the pain in his eyes, which were bleeding freely. He was so overcome that he fainted. For he'd bled so much, and the twisting of his balls made him so faint, that his energy just vanished. Then Reynard the Fox pounced on him with all his strength and caught him by the legs and pulled him across the field of combat so that everyone could see. He then pummeled him.

Isengrim's friends were downcast, and went weeping to the lord their King. They begged him to put a stop to the fight and take it into his own hands. The King granted their request, and so the umpires—the leopard and the lynx—went and addressed the fox and the wolf: "Our lord the King wants to speak with you. He wills that the battle be ended, and that it be taken into his judgment. He judges that you should put the resolution of this fight into his decision. For if either of you were killed here, it would bring shame on both sides. You both have as much honor on the field as you can gain." He then said to the fox: "All the animals who've seen this battle through award the prize to you."

"Then I thank them," replied the fox, "and whatever it pleases my lord to command will be my pleasure to fulfill. I desire nothing better than to have won the field of battle. Let my friends come here to me. I'll take counsel from them as to what I should do. They say that it's wise for a man to take advice from his friends in weighty matters."

Then up came Dame Sloepcade and Grimbart the Badger her husband, Dame Rukenawe with her two sisters, Byteluys and Fulrompe her two sons, and Hatenette her daughter, the bat, and the weasel. They all came, along with more than twenty others who wouldn't have come if the fox had lost. Whoever wins a victory also wins praise and honor. No one comes to the loser.

So the following also came to the fox, all because he'd won: the beaver, the otter, and both their wives Pantecroet and Ordegale, the stoat, the martin, the polecat, the ferret, the mouse, the squirrel, and many more than I can name. Some even came who'd earlier laid charges against the fox. They were now among his closest kin and were extremely friendly toward him. So goes the world these days: whoever is powerful and at the top of Fortune's wheel has many kinsmen and friends, while the indigent and suffering person finds but few friends and kinsmen. Almost every man avoids his company.

They then made a great feast, blowing trumpets and piping with bagpipes. They all said: "Dear nephew, blessed be God that you've won! We were mortally afraid for you when we saw you lying under Isengrim."

The fox thanked them all in a friendly manner and received them joyfully. He then asked them what he should do: Should he give over the judgment to the King or not? Dame Sloepcade said: "Definitely, cousin. You can do this and accrue honor. And you can trust him well enough."

So they all went then with the umpires to the King. Reynard was in front, with trumpets and pipes and minstrelsy of many kinds. The fox knelt before the King, who told him to stand, saying: "Reynard, rejoice! You've won the day with honor. I hereby discharge you and let you go freely wherever you please. I take upon myself resolution of the debate between you and Isengrim. I'll discuss it rationally and with the counsel of my nobles, and will ordain what should be done by justice, when Isengrim has recovered. I'll then summon you, and, by the grace of God, deliver final judgment."

43

The fox offers a parable to the King after he's won the field

"My worthy and dear lord the King: I'm wholly satisfied with your judgment. But when I first entered your court, there were many, who'd never suffered injury at my hand, who were cruel to me and envious of me. They thought they could get the edge on me, and so they all cried out with my enemies against me, and would've happily destroyed me. They did this because they judged that the wolf was in a better place with you than I, your humble subject. They had no other grounds for their action, and didn't reflect as the wise do, thinking how things might turn out in the end.

"My lord, these animals are like a pack of hounds I once saw at a lord's dwelling; they stood beside a dunghill, waiting for men to bring them food. They noticed a dog coming out of the kitchen, who'd stolen a nice rib of beef. He'd have run away quickly, but the cook spotted him before he left, and threw a great bowl of scalding water over the dog's hind parts. The dog wasn't too grateful to the cook for this, because his coat behind was scalded and the skin looked as if it'd been boiled. He nonetheless escaped and kept what he'd won. When his fellows the other hounds saw him go with his delicious rib, they called him and said: 'Oh, how friendly the cook is to you! He's given you such a juicy bone, on which there's so much flesh!'

"The dog replied: 'You don't know what you're talking about. You praise me as if you only see my front. But look behind to my buttocks and you'll see what I paid for this bone.'

"By the time they'd seen his hind parts and the flesh raw and boiled, they all growled and were afraid of the boiling water. They wanted nothing to do with the dog, fleeing from him and leaving him alone.

"Thus, my lord, these unreliable beasts are accustomed, when they've been made lords and have achieved all they want, when they're mighty and feared, to become extortionists. They tax and fleece the people and eat them like starving dogs. They carry the bone in their mouth. No man dares do anything but praise everything they do, and say what will please them, because no man wants to be shorn by scalding. Some help them promote their illegal projects because they want a share too. They lick their fingers and strengthen the wicked in their evil lives and works.

"My dear lord: How little do they see, who only see part of the story! What will become of them? They'll fall shamefully and painfully from high to low and their actions will come to light such that no one will take pity on them in their misery and grief. Many like these have been blamed and shorn very close, gaining no honor or profit, but losing their hair as the dog did, which is to say their friends, who've helped them camouflage their crimes and extortions, just as the hair covers the skin. But when they regret their old crimes, then they withdraw their support and flee, just as the hounds did from the dog that was scalded with the boiling water, leaving the extortionists in their sorrow and need.[44]

"My dear lord the King: I beg you to remember this fable about me—it won't conflict with your honor or wisdom. How many false extortionists do you estimate there are these days—people much worse than a dog who bears a juicy bone in his mouth? In both towns and the courts of the powerful, they aggressively and illegally face the poor down, selling their privileges and freedoms, and deceptively deprive them of things they never knew they had. They do all this to acquire goods for their own selfish advantage. May God bring shame upon them and soon destroy them!

"But, God be thanked," said the fox, "no man may indict me or my kin of this kind of thing. If they do, we'll acquit ourselves, and expose the matter to public view. I'm unafraid of anyone who'll charge me for having acted dishonestly. A fox will always sustain a fox, though all his enemies had sworn to oppose him.

"My dear lord the King, I love you with all my heart above all other lords. I wouldn't turn aside from you for any man. I'll stay by you to the bitter end. However Your Highness has been informed otherwise, I've always done my best by you and will continue to do so, within my utmost power, until the day I die."

44 Reynard's allegory is confused, perhaps deliberately: the scalded dog variously represents both the corrupt and Reynard himself.

PART VIII

The lion king makes Reynard the Fox his most powerful counselor

44

The King forgives the fox everything, and makes him the most powerful lord in all his territory

"eynard, you owe me homage," said the King, "and I hope that you'll continue to pay it forever. I also want you to be a permanent member of my council and one of my justices. Be sure never to err or commit any crime again. I reinstate you to all your power and authority, just as you were before. Be sure to set all matters justly, for when you turn your intelligence and good judgment to virtue and goodness, then our court can't do without your advice and counsel. There's no one here who can match you for penetrating and intelligent counsel, nor in providing more subtle remedies for legal issues. I want you to think about your own fable. Be just and be loyal to me. From now on I'll act by your advice and judgment. Whoever acts against you shall die: I'll avenge it, and you'll be my spokesman everywhere. In all the land you'll be sovereign above all others and stand in for me. I invest you with that office, which you can well occupy honorably."

All Reynard's friends and kin thanked the King profusely. The King said: "I want to do more for your sake than you think. I ask all of you to guide Reynard so that he remains loyal."

Dame Rukenawe then said: "My lord, it'll always be as you say, for sure. Don't think otherwise, for if he acted differently, then he wouldn't belong to our kin or lineage. I'd give him up forever and obstruct him to the utmost of my power."

Reynard the Fox thanked the King eloquently. "Dear lord, I'm unworthy of the honor that you bestow upon me. I'll remain focused on it and be loyal to you as long as I live. I'll give the wisest counsel that will further Your Grace's interests."

With that, he and his friends took their leave of the King.

Now listen to how Isengrim the Wolf acted. Bruin the Bear, Tybert the Cat, and Arswind and her children, along with their kin, pulled the wolf from the field and laid him on a litter of hay. They covered him warmly and tended his wounds, of which there were at least twenty-five. Masters and surgeons came, who bound and washed the wounds. Isengrim was so ill and feeble that he'd lost all sense of feeling. But they rubbed and massaged him under his temples and eyes, so that he rose from his faint and cried so loudly that they were all frightened, thinking he'd lost his wits.

But the doctors administered a potion that comforted him profoundly and made him sleep. They also comforted his wife, telling her that no wound was mortal and that he stood in no danger of dying. The court then broke up and the animals went their separate ways home.

45

The fox and his friends and kin depart nobly from the King and return to Wickedhole

eynard the Fox took his leave of King and Queen with due ceremony. They ordered him not to stay away long, and to return again shortly.

He answered: "Dear King and Queen: I stand forever at your commandment. If you need anything whatsoever, God help me, I'll be at the ready. I'll be prompt to help you with both my body and my property. My friends and kin will also obey your will and command. You've deserved it many times over, and may God repay you both with good grace and long life! I now seek your permission to return home to my wife and children. Should Your Grace desire anything whatsoever, let me know and you'll always find me at the ready."

Thus the fox left the King with an eloquent speech.

The translator takes leave of his book

The translator reflects on how the world is now dominated by foxlike humans

ow, whoever is able to learn Reynard's craftiness, and whoever can use the same flattery and lies, will, I believe, be heard by both spiritual and earthly lords. There are many Reynards these days, including most of those who creep and use holes as he does. The name that was given to him remains forever with him.[45] He's left many heirs of his craftiness in the world. These always grow powerful, because whoever refuses to practice Reynard's craft counts for nothing in the world in any estate that matters. If he's able to creep like Reynard, and has been Reynard's pupil, then he'll prosper with us, because he then knows how to prosper, and is promoted above every competitor.

The world contains many weeds left by Reynard, which now spring up everywhere, even if they have no red beards. There are more foxes found now than ever existed in the past. The righ-

45 The Reynard literary material was so popular in medieval France that the French word for "fox" changed from "goupil" to "reynard" (the word still used in French for "fox").

teous are entirely without hope, now that honesty and justice are in exile. Covetousness, falsehood, hatred, and envy occupy their place. These now reign in every land. For whether it's the court of the Pope, the emperor, the King, the duke, or any other lord whatsoever, everyone works to suppress competitors for honor, offices, and power. Everyone seeks to climb high with strength and force.

Nothing is recognized or loved in court these days except money. Money is loved above God, and men do much more for money than for God. Whoever pays cash will be well received and achieve his aim. Whether it be among lords or ladies or anyone else, money causes profound damage. Money shames many, and causes them to fear for their life. It produces false witnesses against true. It promotes debauchery, lying, and lechery. Clerics and laymen now go to Rome, to Paris, and to many other places to learn Reynard's skills. They all tread in Reynard's footprints, and seek out his hole. That's the way of the world these days—every man always looks out only for himself. How we'll end up, I don't know. Every wise man should grieve at this state of affairs.

Because of the falsehood, theft, robbery, and murder that's now rampant, and for the shameless lechery and adultery boasted and broadcast, I fear that, unless we repent and do penance, God will take vengeance and punish us sorely. I therefore humbly beseech Him from whom nothing is hidden, that He grant us grace to amend and govern ourselves to His pleasure. With that, I take my leave.

For what business do I have to write of these crimes? I've plenty on my plate looking after my own affairs. So it would be better for me to hold my tongue and suffer things as they are, and do the best I can to make amends for myself in the time I have. And so I counsel every man to do likewise in this present life. Action of that kind will bring us the greatest reward, because after this life there's no time left for us to work to our spiritual advantage. At that moment every man will answer for himself and bear his own burden.

Reynard carries on

Reynard's friends and kin, to the number of forty, took leave of the King, and traveled with the fox, who rejoiced that he'd prospered so well and that he stood so well in the King's grace. He judged that he'd incurred no shame, but that he was so intimate with the King that he could promote the interests of his friends and obstruct his enemies. He also thought that he could do whatever he wanted without being blamed, as long as he was clever.

The fox and his friends went together until they came to Wickedhole, where they all took leave of each other eloquently and courteously. Reynard was especially polite to them and thanked them all lovingly for the loyalty and honor that they'd shown toward him. He offered his services, with his body and property, to each if they ever needed him. With that they departed, each going to his own house. The fox went to his wife Dame Ermilyn, who welcomed him warmly. He recounted to her and their children all the amazing things that had befallen him in court. He didn't forget a word, but told them the whole story of his escape. They were glad that their father had been promoted and was so intimate with the King. The fox continued to live with his wife and children in great joy and happiness.

The truth of this story

ow, whoever has said anything about the fox to you, either more or less than you have heard or read here, take it from me: it's a lie. What you've heard or read here, you can believe. Whoever doesn't believe this is mistaken, even if they hadn't seen it, for there are many things in this world that are believed without having been seen. There are also many imagined scenes found here that never happened, which are presented as an example to readers, so that they pursue virtue and avoid sin more readily. The effect of this book might work in this way: whoever reads it, despite the fact that it's full of jokes and funny tricks, may nonetheless find in it a good deal of wisdom and instruction, by which he might more readily come to virtue and honor. No good man is blamed in it. It is expressed generally, without personal attack. Let every man take his own part as he reads it. If anyone find himself guilty in any part of it, let him correct himself. And whoever is truly virtuous, I pray that God keep him in that state. If anything is said or written here that grieves or displeases any man, don't blame me, but blame the fox, for these are his words and not mine. I pray all who read this little treatise to correct and amend it wherever they find fault. I've not added to or subtracted from it, but followed as near as my Dutch original permitted. It was translated by me, William Caxton, into a rough and simple English in Westminster Abbey, being finished on June 6, 1481, the twenty-first year of the reign of King Edward IV.[46]

Here ends the history of Reynard the Fox

46 Edward IV: 1461–70 and 1471–83.

Acknowledgments

This little book was much improved by the acute editorial pen of Bob Weil, whom I warmly acknowledge and thank.

About the Late Fifteenth-Century Translator: William Caxton

(b. 1415–1424; d. 1492)

illiam Caxton holds an extraordinarily important position in British cultural history as the entrepreneur who first introduced a printing press, and thereby the information technology revolution of print, to England.

In 1438 Caxton was apprenticed to a London mercer (a seller of fine cloth). He left England for the Low Countries between 1444 and 1449, to become a merchant adventurer (an English merchant trading internationally). In 1453 he was formally accepted to full membership of the Mercers' Company, by which time he was already active as a businessman in the Low Countries, settling in Bruges. Trade between England and Flanders flourished in the fifteenth century, centered on wool, but also involving many other luxury goods. The extraordinarily prosperous markets of Flanders traded in luxury goods from all over Europe and the wider Mediterranean. Between 1462 and 1470 Caxton served as the governor of the English Nation (the organization representing English commercial interests) in Bruges. The first European publication of a book printed with movable type dates from ca. 1455, with the Gutenberg Bible, printed in

Mainz, Germany. Having learned how to print in Cologne, Caxton published the first printed book in English in 1473–74, a history of Troy that Caxton had himself translated. In 1476 he returned to England, and set up his press at Westminster, where he published the first book in English to be printed in England in 1476. Between this date and his death in 1492, Caxton's printing output was enormous. He translated or edited at least twenty-six books himself; he was also responsible for editions of works by late fourteenth- and fifteenth-century authors Geoffrey Chaucer, John Lydgate, John Tiptoft, and Thomas Malory.[47]

47 For Caxton's career, see N. F. Blake, *Caxton and His World* (London: André Deutsch, 1969).

About the Early Twenty-first-Century Translator: James Simpson (b. 1954)

James Simpson is the Donald P. and Katherine B. Loker Professor of English at Harvard University (2004–). Formerly a professor of medieval and Renaissance English at the University of Cambridge, he is an Honorary Fellow of the Australian Academy of the Humanities. His secondary education was at Scotch College Melbourne, Australia. His tertiary education was at the Universities of Melbourne and Oxford. His most recent books are *Reform and Cultural Revolution*, being volume 2 in the *Oxford English Literary History* (Oxford University Press, 2002), *Burning to Read: English Fundamentalism and Its Reformation Opponents* (Harvard University Press, 2007), and *Under the Hammer: Iconoclasm in the Anglo-American Tradition* (Oxford University Press, 2010). He is a co-editor of the *Norton Anthology of English Literature.*